An End of Night

A Shade of Vampire, Book 16

Bella Forrest

ALSO BY BELLA FORREST:

A SHADE OF VAMPIRE SERIES:

Derek & Sofia's story:

A Shade of Vampire (Book 1)
A Shade of Blood (Book 2)
A Castle of Sand (Book 3)
A Shadow of Light (Book 4)
A Blaze of Sun (Book 5)
A Gate of Night (Book 6)
A Break of Day (Book 7)

Rose & Caleb's story:

A Shade of Novak (Book 8)
A Bond of Blood (Book 9)
A Spell of Time (Book 10)
A Chase of Prey (Book 11)
A Shade of Doubt (Book 12)
A Turn of Tides (Book 13)
A Dawn of Strength (Book 14)
A Fall of Secrets (Book 15)

A SHADE OF KIEV TRILOGY:

A Shade of Kiev 1
A Shade of Kiev 2
A Shade of Kiev 3

BEAUTIFUL MONSTER DUOLOGY:

Beautiful Monster 1
Beautiful Monster 2

For an updated list of Bella's books,
please visit www.bellaforrest.net

Contents

Chapter 1: Sofia

"We need to break Lilith's heart."

After Mona had said the words, we all looked around at each other in confusion.

"Break Lilith's heart?" I asked. "What do you mean? How?"

"I don't know," Mona said. "We need to find Magnus and speak to him, learn more about Lilith and figure out what would hurt her the most."

"Even if we somehow do manage to find him," Ashley said, "what makes you think he would want to help us? What if he still loves her?"

"He needs to understand what the black witches are

doing now," Mona said. "Their plan, if successful, will mean that no species, no realm, is safe—except perhaps the dragons. And we need to tell him about the bond Lilith formed between them to keep her alive this long. My guess is that he isn't even aware of it."

"If Lilith is as horrifying as Mona makes out," Kiev muttered, "one look at her should be enough to break whatever attachment remains."

"So we would have to find Magnus and then take him to Lilith," Xavier said. "Do we even know where Lilith is?"

"I have some ideas," Mona replied. "You can leave that to me. The first thing we need to do is find Magnus and persuade him to cooperate."

"Where would we even start?" I asked. "We know for sure that he is still alive since Lilith is, but in theory couldn't he be anywhere within the human or supernatural realms?"

Mona nodded. "It's going to be one hell of a task. I'm going to try taking another memory potion to see if I can glean any more information about Magnus, but in case I can't…" She turned to her husband, placing a hand on his shoulder. "Kiev, what else do you remember about the man? Please, try to think."

Kiev furrowed his brows, running a hand across his forehead. "I don't know," he said after a long pause. "As I mentioned, I barely knew him. I just remember him stopping by briefly at The Blood Keep many, many centuries ago."

Eli looked up from the laptop in front of him. His expression was grim.

"There have been several more mass kidnappings already," he said. "Just shy of one thousand humans have been reported missing now."

I wondered if the government authorities had bothered to listen to us about closing schools and warning everyone. Whatever the case, our efforts obviously hadn't deterred the black witches.

Mona drew a breath. "Almost one thousand," she said. "I can't imagine much more blood will be needed now until they are ready...We are running out of time. Fast."

Chapter 2: Rose

I kissed Caleb until the corners of my mouth felt sore. He had been crouched over me as we lay on the jetty, his body pressed against me as he claimed my lips over and over. I ran my hands through his hair while he lifted himself off me and lay down beside me. I raised my right hand, examining the exquisite ring he'd given me.

Engaged. That's what I am now.

I was still in shock. One minute I had been dancing with Caleb, and the next he had gone down on one knee and pulled out a ring. It all felt so surreal.

He turned on his side and pulled me closer to him until my nose was barely an inch away from his.

"Rose Achilles," he said softly.

His voice and the way he looked at me made my nerves tingle. My body heated up. I pressed myself closer against him, as close as I could get. I felt his chest tense as I kissed his jawline. I nuzzled my head against him.

"And how long do I have to wait until you make me fully yours?" I asked in a whisper.

He placed his hand over my forehead, tilting my head back so he could look me directly in the eye. He smiled, then sat up abruptly, pulling me up with him. My heart raced as he held me in his arms and stood up. Expecting him to start running toward our cabin, I reached for his shirt and began unbuttoning it.

To my disappointment, he headed in the opposite direction, toward the beach.

Once we had exited the Port and arrived just a few feet away from the beginning of the waves, he put me down. He held my hands in his, bending his head down to face me. I looked up at him, my eyes wide with expectation— even though I'd already guessed the words he was about to speak.

"We have waited this long already… I think we should wait for our wedding night."

My stomach sank. "We could do that," I said, trying to hide my disappointment, "or we could go back to our room now…"

His smile broadened. "It will be all the more special if

we wait," he said. He leaned toward me, brushing his lips against my neck, before whispering into my ear: "I promise."

"And how long until our wedding?" I asked.

"Your guess is as good as mine," he said. "I don't think anyone on this island is up for another wedding while the threat of Lilith remains hanging over everyone."

I sighed. "I know."

Yet another reason for wanting to end that hag as soon as possible.

"Speaking of Lilith," I said, "I wonder if Mona might have returned by now."

We began making our way back toward the Residences. We'd almost reached them when Caleb stopped.

"I hear voices coming from the Great Dome," he said.

"Let's head there."

We arrived outside the Great Dome and pushed open the doors. Sitting around the long table were my parents, grandfather, uncle and aunt, and all the members of our council except for Claudia and Yuri.

I was relieved to spot Mona sitting next to Kiev. Caleb and I sat down in the nearest spare seats.

"What is happening?" I asked.

"Caleb," Mona said, ignoring my question. "Do you know of a man—a vampire—called Magnus?"

"Magnus," Caleb said, looking surprised. "Magnus

who?"

"We don't know," she replied. "But a vampire named Magnus is the key to ending Lilith once and for all. I know only a little about the man from accessing Lilith's memories with the help of a potion. I just spent an hour trying to access more, but it seems I've already witnessed all that she unwittingly shared with me."

"I did know of a Magnus," Caleb said slowly. "Wasn't he a child of the Elders? I saw him briefly in Cruor."

Mona's eyes widened. "You knew a vampire named Magnus in Cruor?"

"I didn't *know* him. He wasn't a prisoner there like the rest of us were. He was a child of the Elders. He was freer than us, more privileged. He could come and go as he pleased, or so it seemed. I never talked much with him."

"It must be the same Magnus," Kiev said. "There can't have been two children of the Elders named Magnus. Do you know what happened to him, Caleb?"

Caleb shook his head. "I remember him because there was a short period when he brought us blood every day. Then he just stopped coming and was replaced by someone else. I have no idea what happened to him."

"Well, none of this helps us," Xavier said. "It would have been a long time ago that Caleb saw him there. And he left. We have no idea where he might be now."

Kiev stood up abruptly, looking around at everyone in

the room. "Let's go to The Blood Keep."

"The Blood Keep?" several vampires asked at once.

"Why?" my father asked. "It was centuries ago that you saw him there. What makes you think that—"

"Oh, I don't expect to find him there," Kiev replied. "But there is something in that castle that I believe might help us."

"Didn't we ransack The Blood Keep decades ago?" Zinnia said.

"The building might still be standing," Kiev said.

My father stood up, followed by my mother.

I was still confused as to what everyone was talking about. Who was Magnus? Why was he the end of Lilith? Clearly, nobody was in the mood to answer my questions now.

"Okay," my father said. "We leave for The Blood Keep."

Several people were looking doubtfully at Kiev, but it didn't seem that anyone had any brighter ideas.

"Xavier and Vivienne, you will stay here in The Shade. The rest of us can go. Ibrahim and Corrine, we will need you, obviously." Everyone stood up, including Caleb and me. I was waiting for my parents to tell me that I should stay too, but they didn't bother. It seemed that they were past trying to keep me out of things.

"Be careful," Vivienne said, her hands resting over her stomach.

"The dragons will remain with you too," my father said. "The rest of you can come. Though I'd prefer we keep our party no larger than fifteen members. We will be back as soon as we can." He kissed his sister on the forehead, then nodded toward Xavier before following us all out of the Dome.

Fifteen of us gathered in the clearing outside: Caleb and me, my parents, grandfather, Kiev and Mona, Corrine and Ibrahim, Kiev's siblings and Matteo, Micah, Ashley and Landis. My mother was looking worriedly at me. She walked over and held my hand. A small gasp escaped her lips when she realized that I was wearing a ring. She stared at it, looked from me to Caleb, then back to me.

"You're engaged?" she choked.

I nodded, grinning. Tears brimmed in her eyes. My father was already in conversation with Corrine and Ibrahim, but my mother caught his hand and pulled him over. She pointed to my ring.

Despite the worry creasing my father's forehead, he couldn't hold back a smile. He drew me in and planted a tender kiss on my head. Then he placed a hand on Caleb's shoulder. "Congratulations," he said, his voice hoarse.

"Derek?" Ibrahim called.

My father left to continue talking. My mother hugged me tightly. I felt her shake slightly, as though she was trying to suppress a sob.

"Sofia," my father called.

She let go of me and joined him. I moved closer to Caleb, wrapping my arms around him. After a couple of minutes, my parents, Ibrahim, and Corrine had finished their conversation. They turned to the rest of us.

"Let's go," my father said. "Form a circle."

We all gathered around and did as requested.

"Corrine and Ibrahim are going to take us directly within the compound of The Blood Keep. We don't know what we are going to find there now, so be careful once we arrive."

My parents took their place in the circle next to me. My father held one of my hands, while Caleb held the other, and we all vanished.

CHAPTER 3: SOFIA

Even as we arrived outside the looming castle and crossed the shadowy courtyard, all I could think about was my daughter being engaged. I couldn't believe how fast she had grown up. It still seemed like just yesterday I'd been nursing her in my arms. *My baby girl.*

I was knocked back to reality as Derek and Kiev pushed open the ancient oak doors. A strong smell of decay wafted out from the building. We walked through the door into the entry hall. I shuddered as I took in the place. It looked much the same as I remembered it. Long velvet curtains hid the windows and the high ceilings were covered with cobwebs. There was a thick layer of dust coating the floor. Looking around, it appeared that nobody had stepped in here since the day the Elder had escaped with his vampires through the portal. A portal that was supposed to have been closed by the late Ageless.

Remembering that Derek was no longer a vampire and couldn't see in the dark, I gripped his arm and led him forward as we crossed the hallway. We stopped at the base of the wide staircase leading up. All eyes turned toward Kiev.

"So?" Mona said, her voice echoing eerily around the hall. "Why did you bring us all here?"

Kiev looked paler than usual, his eyes haunted with memories. It seemed to take a moment for him to compose himself enough to answer. "While I was staying here," he said, his voice deep, "there was a room where the name of every single one of the Elder's children was recorded. On the walls… It was a job my Elder had given Clara. We need to find that room. I don't remember exactly where it is now."

"Where do we start?" Derek asked.

"Upstairs," Kiev replied.

I remained holding onto Derek as we climbed the stairs. I looked back to see Caleb supporting Rose.

The first floor was brighter than the ground floor. Many of the curtains were either torn or ripped right from the rails, allowing the rays of the moon to shine through. Derek didn't need me to guide him anymore.

This level was also more wrecked than the floor below—pieces of crushed furniture and shards of glass from smashed mirrors were scattered everywhere. Perhaps this floor was where the main battle had taken place that night Derek and our vampires had stormed the castle in search of me.

"I suggest we split up to make this faster," Derek said.

"What exactly are we looking for?" Matteo asked.

"One wall, covered with etchings of names," Kiev replied.

Half of us split right, while the other half went left. Even as a vampire, I found myself shivering as I walked along the corridors and looked in each of the rooms. Many of them I recognized from my stay here, and when I reached the room at the end of the corridor I was walking along, I stood rooted to the spot. It was all too familiar. I gulped, looking around, and stopped at the foot of the bed. This had been the chamber I had been imprisoned in while I was pregnant with the twins.

Someone entered behind me. Kiev.

"Oh, you're already checking in here," he muttered. He stopped short as he realized which room this was. All the emotions—the fear, the uncertainty, the distrust—I'd held for the vampire during my stay within these walls came back to me full force. I remembered how much his erratic, violent and unpredictable nature had terrorized me. I had begun to believe that I would never make it out of this place alive. If it weren't for Shadow, I probably wouldn't have.

Our eyes met across the room. His expression was dark, tortured. It was hard to believe that the same vampire who'd kept me captive was standing before me now.

"Kiev," Mona called from outside the door. She stepped inside, looking at the two of us. "Derek thinks he has found it."

We both snapped out of our bout of nostalgia and followed Mona out of the room. We hurried along the corridor, then took a right into a small chamber. Despite its size, everyone had piled in and was staring at the wall opposite the door. Kiev made his way to the front of the group and stared at the wall. Sure enough, it was covered with names.

"This is it," he said, running a hand down the rough wall. "We need to try to find Magnus listed here…"

The next two minutes passed in silence as we all scanned the old, barely legible, etchings in the stone. It was Rose who was the first to call out, "I think this is it." Squatting, she squinted at a name etched particularly low down on the wall. "Magnus Helios."

"Helios," Kiev repeated slowly. He stood up and leaned against the wall, raising a hand to his head and rubbing his temples. He closed his eyes, frowning in concentration.

"Why is that surname familiar to me?" he said, more to himself than to anyone else.

We all waited with bated breath, watching as Kiev racked his brain. When he finally did look up, he appeared to be uncomfortable. He glanced at Mona.

She raised her brows. "What?"

"Long before I met you, I had a brief affair with a woman—a vampire—called Ernesta Helios." He shifted on his feet. "It happened during a visit I paid to the coven in Amsterdam—The Underground. Given the Elders' penchant for going after people of the same bloodline"—he nodded toward Helina and Erik across the room—"it's no stretch of imagination to conclude that Magnus and Ernesta are related. Of course, at the time I had no idea. Talking was something Ernesta and I didn't do much of."

"She's not listed here on the wall," Derek said, frowning.

"No," Kiev said, "she wasn't a direct child of the Elders."

"Ernesta Helios," Matteo muttered.

We all turned to look at the Italian vampire.

"I knew that vampire, too," he said. "She lives in The Tavern. Or at least, she did when I was there last."

"The Tavern?" Derek asked. "What is The Tavern?"

"It is an island in the supernatural realm," Matteo replied. "An island founded by a group of outcasts. Over the years, it has become a place of respite for all those in the supernatural realm who have either left or been rejected from their own homes."

"Matteo," Derek said. "What is the likelihood that Ernesta is still there on that island?"

Matteo shrugged. "She was a permanent resident there when I last visited. I don't see a reason why she wouldn't still be there now."

We all exchanged glances. Mona looked more uneasy than ever.

"If we are seriously contemplating going all the way to The Tavern," she said, "we had better hope that this doesn't turn out to be a wild-goose chase."

Chapter 4: Rhys

I stopped outside the red door. Reaching for the handle, I paused, taking a deep breath. I could hear sounds coming from within—Isolde and Julisse, no doubt.

"Come in, Rhys," my aunt called.

I pushed open the door and stepped inside. The two women were standing around a giant vat fixed in the center of the chamber. It was filled to the brim with blood, and steam was billowing up from it. This was just a small portion of the blood we had collected over the last few days.

"We have enough for the first part of the ritual," Isolde said.

I raised a brow. "Are you certain?"

"Yes," Isolde said. "You should bring Lilith here now. We have finished draining the blood from all the humans needed for the ritual. This is the last batch. Go now. We are ready."

I nodded and glanced once more at the blood before leaving the room. Closing the door behind me, I began walking slowly along the corridor.

Lilith. She had been furious that we had failed to take hold of The Shade. At least now, finally, we had some good news for her. I stopped at the end of the hallway and looked out of the window, watching the glistening waves crash against the island. Then I vanished myself.

A few seconds later, I was standing on a black pebble stone beach, facing the same dark ocean. I turned around and made my way up to the entrance of Lilith's cave. I passed through the dimly lit tunnels and arrived in the circular chamber.

"Lilith," I called, fixing my eyes on the still black pool in the center of the room.

No response. I reached the edge of the pool and continued to call her name. Still no answer. I was about to dip my hand in and disturb the liquid when a rasping voice called from behind me.

"Rhys."

I whirled around to see Lilith's skeletal body descending a flight of stairs. Her legs looked shaky as she made her way toward me. I bowed my head in greeting. I was surprised and anxious to see her out of her pool of liquid.

"I sensed you would be arriving any time now," she said, her beady black eyes narrowing on me.

"We are ready to complete the first part of the ritual. It's time for you to come with me."

"Are you certain you have enough blood?"

"Yes, we are certain we have enough. We also tried to collect mostly females, because we know this is your preference."

"Young or old blood?"

"Mostly young," I replied.

She clucked her tongue, nodding slowly in approval. "Follow me then." A second later she had vanished from the spot.

I followed quickly after her, unsure of what part of our castle she would reappear in. I manifested again outside the main entrance, but she was nowhere in sight. I transported myself to the spell room. She stood by the boiling vat of blood next to my aunt and my sister.

I exchanged glances with the two of them before addressing Lilith. "Allow us to take you outside. We need space."

Julisse and Isolde stopped stirring the blood and gripped the vessel. The four of us left the spell room and reappeared outside the castle among a cluster of rocks. Julisse led the way, the vat of blood hovering above our heads, and stopped at the edge of a wide pool that had been dug into the ground, already almost filled with blood. Julisse and Isolde tipped the remaining blood into the pool and discarded the vessel, hurling it several feet away from us where it landed with a clatter.

Lilith's gaze was fixed on the blood. Slowly she lowered herself to the ground, sat on the edge of the pool and slid into the liquid. She submerged herself completely, then surfaced again, her rotten flesh now tinged with red.

My aunt looked my way. "Fetch the others while I begin preparation."

I transported myself back into the castle, appearing in the main entrance hall where all of our companions were waiting patiently, as instructed. I needed to give them but a nod before they understood. They vanished with me and we all reappeared back outside around the pool of blood.

Lilith's eyes traveled around the crowd as we all formed a circle around her.

Isolde looked at everyone sternly. "You all understand your parts in this?" she asked.

Everyone nodded in response.

"Then we begin."

As soon as my aunt had spoken the words, Lilith dipped back down into the blood, out of sight.

Isolde then began to chant. We followed her as she led,

starting out slowly, then building in pace and volume until I could barely hear my own voice amidst the others around me. I closed my eyes in concentration, allowing no thoughts to enter, focusing only on the words coming from my mouth.

After an hour of chanting, I could feel heat beginning to emanate from the pool. I opened my eyes slightly to see that the blood was beginning to swirl and churn. Lilith was still nowhere in sight. I closed my eyes again, clenching my fists. Now was the most crucial part of this ritual. None of us could let up on our concentration.

I only opened my eyes once again when there was a loud splash and Isolde's voice quietened. I took a step back, staring in awe at the sight unfolding before us. The figure of a woman was hovering in the air above the pool. She wore Lilith's ragged clothes, but gone was any sign of the Ancient's rotting corpse. The clothes hung off a young, shapely body, the body of a young woman with long dark hair and pale skin. Her eyes were shut tight as she whirled around and around in the air, her arms folded across her chest, her legs intertwined with each other.

By now, we had all stopped chanting. As she began to move toward me, I stepped aside, allowing her to float past me. She lowered to the ground. Her body was still and limp against the rocks as she touched down. Her eyes were still closed, a frown creasing her smooth forehead. Isolde hurried over and bent down over her, wiping away the blood from her face and feeling her pulse.

After a minute, she looked around at the rest of us. "Lilith has returned with the strength of her youth."

CHAPTER 5: ROSE

Mona consulted the map she had brought with us. She traced her finger along the various gate locations until she settled on one at a nearby shore.

"I'm not sure where this one leads," she said, "but it'll have to be good enough for now. Everyone, gather around Ibrahim, Corrine and me."

"Wait," I said. "Don't you think we should return to The Shade and bring at least one dragon with us, just for good measure?"

Mona scowled. "Those beasts refuse to be transported by magic. It would take too long to fly to the gate. We will have to do without them."

"Okay," I mumbled nervously.

We made sure we were all touching each other. The room disappeared and a few seconds later, we found ourselves at the top of a mountain with a view of the ocean far in the distance. A volcano, I soon realized. There was a deep crater about twenty feet away from us and heat emanated from the rocks, seeping into the soles of my feet and warming my whole body.

We all looked toward Mona. She had a look of confusion on her face. We all moved closer to the crater to see a bed of molten lava beneath it. Steam billowed upward, scalding our faces. Mona stumbled back, looking back down at the map. "There's supposed to be a gate here," she said.

"There's another hole over there," Micah—in his wolf form—said, his eyes fixed on a spot in the distance.

We moved over to the hole—partially obscured by the huge crater in front of us—and gathered round it. Sure enough, there was no lava. Just the starry crater that indicated a portal into the supernatural world.

We didn't delay in leaping through. Spiraling down through the vacuum, I braced myself to shoot out the other end and land on the ground—wherever it might be. But to my surprise, it wasn't land that greeted me at the other end. I was thrust into a body of cool water.

I closed my mouth, kicking hard upward. I made it to the surface and looked around. Caleb appeared next to me a few moments later, as did the rest of the group. Surrounding us was nothing but open sea. Thankfully, it was nighttime. A full moon shone overhead, the sky glittering with thousands of stars.

"Strange," Mona muttered. She looked back down into the depths we had just emerged from.

"What's strange?" Aiden asked.

"That the Ancients should drill a portal right in the depths of the ocean," she answered. "Oh…" Her voice trailed off as she looked at the soggy map still clasped in her fingers. "I guess this map won't be of much use this side of the gates anyway. We're going to have to hope that either I can remember how to get back to the spot, or we find another gate to travel back to the human realm. Now, let's try to get to The Tavern."

We made sure we were all touching, and then the scene around us disappeared. We reappeared not in water this time, but on a sandy beach. Laughter and chatter filled the air. Once my vision came into focus, there was a high wall that stretched as far as I could see. An orange glow emanated from behind the wall, and occasional billows of smoke.

"It's bizarre to be back here," Matteo muttered. He looked toward Kiev. "You had better make him invisible," he said to Mona. "If he is recognized, they will want his head."

"Good idea," Mona said beneath her breath. She vanished Kiev.

Mona and Matteo walked in front, and we followed them up to a tall wooden door built into the wall. Stopping before it, Mona knocked. We waited in silence, then footsteps approached. The door creaked open and a hideous-looking creature appeared behind it—an ogre. He had one eye missing and the other gleamed bright orange.

His jaw dropped as he laid eyes on Mona and Matteo before looking over the rest of us. "Where have you two been?" he asked.

"No time now, Ronan," Mona said, "I'm afraid that we are in a rush. May we enter?"

He stepped aside, and we all piled in through the door, stepping into a small brick enclosure. "What are you here for?" the ogre asked, closing the door behind us.

"We are looking to speak to a vampire named Ernesta Helios," Matteo said. "I believe she resides here?"

"Ernesta," the ogre muttered. "Yes. We have a vampire of that name here."

"Where does she live?" Matteo asked.

"The vampire quarters," Ronan replied. "But I'm not sure that she will be home at this time of night. You might want to look around the town center for her before visiting her home. She's usually out about now."

"Okay, thanks," Mona said.

The ogre's eyes remained on us as we followed Mona up a flight of stairs. Climbing up the steps, we appeared out in the open—clearly the borders of a makeshift town. Shabby buildings made of logs and bricks lined a wide dirt street. The place was lit with lanterns hanging from trees that gave off a warm glow. Various creatures milled about: mostly vampires, werewolves and ogres, and some I didn't even recognize. Quite a few of them looked like they had survived some kind of battle. They had physical impairments—some were missing legs or arms, while others looked unstable as they walked, being supported by walking sticks.

"As I said," Mona said quietly, eyeing a werewolf with a missing hind leg sitting several feet away beneath a tree, "this is an island of outcasts—creatures who were rejected by their own kind. This is where they find their refuge. As for Ernesta, I suspect she came here because she was on the run from the Elders."

"Makes sense," a voice muttered a few feet away from me—Kiev's voice.

I continued observing this strange town as we walked further into its center. Creatures stared back at us curiously, but nobody came up to speak to us, although Mona and Matteo did wave to some of them—old friends, I guessed.

We stopped outside a large stone building with a sign above the entrance that read "The Blue Tavern".

"This pub is a good place to start," Mona said. "You should all wait outside while I go in to see Elizabeth."

Since the front door to the pub was in constant use, we stepped aside so as not to be in the way. Mona reappeared moments later shaking her head. "Ernesta is not in there. Elizabeth advised to try the main square. Apparently that's where a lot of vampires gather at this time of night."

We left the pub and wound our way along the streets until we reached a clearing where crowds of vampires were gathered—some sitting around on wooden benches, others standing in clusters talking. Mona walked up to the nearest vampire to us, a short man with a bald head. "Is there a vampire here called Ernesta Helios?" she asked politely.

"Ernesta," he said, turning to scan the area. "She is over there." He pointed toward a cluster of females in the far right corner.

"Which one is she?" Mona asked.

"The tallest among them," he said. "Short dark hair…"

With that, he turned his back on Mona and continued his conversation. As I looked over at the group he had indicated, I could already spot a vampire of that description.

"Ah yes, I see her," Matteo said. "Ernesta," he said in a raised voice as we approached but a few feet away from the group.

The tall woman with short dark hair turned her blue

eyes on us. They widened as she spotted Matteo.

"Matteo?" she said. "What brings you here?"

He eyed the women surrounding Ernesta. "Could I have a word?"

"Uh, all right." She looked curiously at each of us before turning to her companions. "I will see you in a bit. Where would you like to speak?" she asked Matteo.

"Your home would probably be best."

"I doubt all of you will fit inside. You know how small it is."

"That's fine," Matteo said. "We don't all need to come inside. And hopefully, we won't be long."

No further words were exchanged. She led us away from the square and back along the narrow streets. She stopped outside a rickety-looking two-story cottage. Pushing open the door, she held it open for Matteo to step inside, followed by Mona—then the invisible Kiev—then my parents, grandfather, Caleb, me, Helina and Erik. The rest waited outside. Ernesta led us through the dark hallway into a small sitting room. There weren't enough seats for all of us to sit down, so most of us remained standing.

"Well?" Ernesta said, folding her hands over her lap.

"You can remove the invisibility spell now, Mona." Kiev spoke a few feet away.

Ernesta's jaw dropped as Kiev appeared. "Kiev?"

The vampire took a seat between Matteo and Mona.

"What on earth are you doing here?" She looked toward the door, as if checking that it was shut. "You are considered a criminal here, you do realize that, don't you? Do you have any idea the punishment that would befall me for abetting someone like you? I could be kicked out of this place."

"As Matteo said, we won't be long." Kiev leaned forward in his seat. "We need to know where your brother is."

"What?"

"Where is Magnus?" Kiev's eyes blazed into hers.

"I have no idea where my brother is," she said, exasperation in her tone.

"When was the last time you saw him?" Matteo asked.

She clasped a palm to her forehead. "My... it was many, many years ago. I can't even remember how long it's been. I've lost track. You see, my brother and I had a falling out. We parted ways due to... irreconcilable differences. "

"What differences?" Mona asked .

The vampire frowned. "That's a little too personal for me to feel comfortable discussing in front of strangers."

"Ernesta," Kiev said, standing up and walking over to her seat. "We need to find your brother. Do you have any idea where he could be now?"

"Why do you need to find him?" she asked.

Kiev exchanged glances with Mona and Matteo, then turned back to Ernesta. "Are you aware that your brother was in love with an Ancient?"

Ernest shook her head. "No. I had no idea… Even when we were in touch, we were never close enough to discuss romantic relationships."

"Are you aware of the situation with the black witches?" Matteo pressed.

"I have been out of touch with affairs going on outside of this island."

"Well, now is the time to enlighten yourself," Mona said impatiently, also standing. "They are attempting to carry out a ritual that has never been done before. If successful, it would have catastrophic consequences not just for humans, but all species too weak to fight off their powers. Even The Tavern would not be safe. Lilith—the Ancient your brother was in love with—is a key part of this ritual they are trying to carry out. We need to end her before they can complete it—"

"I still don't understand why you need my brother."

"He is the reason Lilith is still alive. She loved him deeply, madly, and it's that bond of love that is keeping her hanging on. We must find him so he can help us break it."

Ernesta's lips parted in disbelief as she took in Mona's words. This was the first time I had heard a full explanation about why we needed Magnus, so I was grateful that Mona had explained it.

"I see," Ernesta said, swallowing hard. "Well, the last I

heard of my brother, he was residing in The Cove."

"The realm of the mermaids," Mona muttered. "But you have no idea if he might still be there now?"

She shook her head. "I'm sorry. I can only suggest that you travel there and ask if anyone there knows where he is. Even if he isn't there, perhaps you will be able to pick up his trail. I'm sure they would be able to give you more insight about Magnus than I can, in any case."

"When Mona and I were last near those shores," Kiev said, "the Hawks had taken over the merpeople's land. Do you know if this is still the case?"

"Oh, no," Ernesta replied. "At least, the rumor is that the Hawks were forced to retreat from The Cove in order to return to their own realm, Aviary. They needed all the reinforcements they could get in their war with the Elders."

"Do you know what the outcome of that war was?" my mother asked. "Or is it still ongoing?"

"It was brutal," Ernesta said. "They attacked each other's realms so fiercely and weakened each other's resources to such an extent that neither side is much of a force to be reckoned with anymore. The Elders finished off huge numbers of Hawks and destroyed many of their natural resources, while an army of Hawks managed to penetrate Cruor and destroy their supply of human blood and vessels."

"I see," my mother said. "Thank you for that

information."

"Now, is there anything else you could tell us about your brother that might help in tracking him down?" Matteo asked.

Ernesta bit her lower lip. "There's not a lot I can tell you of his past that would be relevant now, because it was so long ago. But I can warn you, if you do manage to find him… be careful. My brother can be… unpredictable."

With that, she stood up and looked toward the door, indicating that we were now at risk of overstaying our welcome.

Mona, Matteo and Kiev looked dissatisfied, as all of us were, but it seemed Ernesta was done offering information. Mona made Kiev invisible again before we all exited the sitting room, walked along the hallway and bundled out onto the street outside.

"Good luck," Ernesta said, eyeing us one last time before shutting her door.

"What happened?" Ibrahim asked.

"She couldn't tell us much," Mona replied. "Last she knew of her brother, he was in The Cove."

Ashley heaved a sigh. "So now what? We've got to travel to The Cove?"

"It's the only lead we have," my father replied.

"Hey, Mona! Matteo!" a gravelly voice called behind us.

We whirled around to see a gray wolf running toward

us. As he neared, I realized that he was missing an ear.

"Oh, hello, Edward," Mona murmured.

"I haven't seen you around in a long time," the wolf said. "What have you been up to?"

"Too much," Matteo said.

Edward chuckled. "We're having a roast out on the beach tonight," he said. "Why don't you join us? Ronan's wife is cooking and there will be blood, too."

"Very tempting," Matteo replied, "but we are just passing through. We have to leave now. Thank you for the invitation, in any case."

"Suit yourself," Edward said. "It's good to see you both. Hopefully we can catch up one of these days."

"Thank you," Mona replied. "Enjoy dinner."

Once the wolf had bounded away, Mona and Matteo turned to us. "Okay," Mona said. "Let's get out of here before there are any more distractions."

Chapter 6: Rose

A strong sea wind whipped against my skin when our feet hit solid ground again. When I looked around, we were all standing on a small rock formation. Its surface was covered with a slimy moss-like substance and was uneven, dipping now and then to form shallow pools. My stomach churned as I caught sight of a massive spider crab about a foot away from where I was standing. I clutched Caleb's arm and squeezed it.

"Gross," I breathed, pointing to the creature.

Caleb looked amused by my reaction. "There are plenty more where that came from." He gestured toward a mound about a hundred yards to our left. It was swarming with crabs scuttling in and out, carrying what looked like oysters and small fish between their razor-sharp pincers.

"Those things are fierce," I said.

"Hunter crabs," Caleb replied.

"Well I don't want them hunting me," I muttered.

"You had better toughen up, Rose," Mona said darkly. "Those crabs are the prettiest things you are going to see while we're here in The Cove. I promise you that."

I shuddered.

After everything I had been through, all the horrors I had seen, one would have thought that I would have overcome my fear of spidery creatures. Now I wasn't sure I would ever overcome it.

Ashley gripped Landis' arm none too gently as she eyed a couple of crabs near her. She stumbled out of the way as they started scuttling straight for her.

At least I'm not the only one.

I'd been too occupied with the crabs until now and hadn't looked properly at our surroundings. Beyond the small rock formation we were standing on was ocean, and further still, all around us were clusters of countless more islets, spreading out as far as we could see. The Cove, it seemed, was one massive, sprawling archipelago. Still gripping Caleb tightly in case I slipped, I moved toward the edge of the rocks and stared down. The water was dark and murky, and was tinged a dark green from the dense sea flora growing within it.

"Okay," Mona said. "Listen up, everyone. We need to tread very carefully. We can't afford to have anyone slipping into these waters."

"What would happen if one of us did fall?" I couldn't help but ask.

"Just don't. Inside the archipelago, these waters are the merfolk's private property. It's simply not done. We're going to have to try to get someone's attention while we are up on these rocks. Merfolk are hostile enough as it is. We need to try to extract information from them about Magnus, and any of us falling in might prove to be a fatal blow to any chance we have. So just… watch your step."

"So what now?" Micah asked. His claws were extended, digging into the moss to keep his hold on the ground, and his paws were sopping wet.

"We're going to travel from islet to islet, using magic of course," Mona said. "And we all need to scan the waters surrounding us. Tell me if you see anything."

With that, we all cautiously began spreading out toward the edge of the islet. I could still see nothing but murky green as Caleb and I made our way around the islet. It didn't take long for all of us to finish scoping out the rocks. Mona magicked us to the next rock formation and we continued our search.

Perhaps it was just my imagination, but there seemed to be even more crabs on this island. It was hard to concentrate on the waters when I was constantly checking my feet to see if one was scuttling over me. I ended up admitting defeat and climbing onto Caleb's back.

"Whoa," my mother said behind us. Caleb hurried over to her with me. She was pointing toward the waves. The water churned violently, and as I strained my eyes, I could make out an enormous black shape.

"It's a shark," Corrine said.

"If you're right, that is one long-ass shark," Ashley murmured.

Corrine was right. A shiny fin protruded above the surface before sinking back down again seconds later.

"Just another reason why nobody should go slipping into these waters," Mona said.

Once we had finished that second islet, we moved on to a third. This time it was Caleb and I who spotted something strange in the water. At first I thought it was some kind of long red stringy flora, but then it began to move and swirl. Caleb caught sight of a pulsating oblong object the same color as the stringy things, which turned out to be giant tentacles. The creature moved backward in one sudden motion.

"A squid?" I gasped.

"Looks like it," Caleb said.

The others came over to look at what we had spotted.

"Yes, a squid," Matteo said.

"Everything here is supersized," Ashley said.

"Let's keep moving," Mona said.

We reached the fourth islet. Here we spotted black-striped sea serpents gliding through the water. I looked around at the seemingly never-ending archipelago. "How long is it going to take us?" I said, more to myself than to anyone else.

"We're going to have to hope that we spot some merfolk sooner rather than later," Mona said.

We were about to move on to the fifth islet when a shrill scream broke through the calm. I turned in time to see Helina flying backward, a bright red tentacle wrapped around her waist. She was pulled off the rocks and out of sight. There was a splash.

"No!" Matteo, Kiev and Erik yelled at once.

The three men were a blur as they raced toward the edge and dove into the water after Helina.

"No!" Mona shouted. We all rushed to the edge and looked down. None of them were visible—all we could see were ripples in the murky water where they had disappeared.

Biting her trembling lip, Mona faced Corrine and Ibrahim. "Hover over the water with me and help me create a whirlpool."

The three witches floated off the rocks with their palms facing downward. The sea beneath them began to churn, slowly at first, but quickly gathering momentum until a swirling vortex of water had formed. We all stared down into the eye of the whirlpool. I spotted the redness of the squid showing in the wall of water. Then Helina's scream echoed upward. The tentacle was still wrapped around her waist, and no matter how much she clawed at it, it wouldn't let go. I caught sight of the shadow of the three men in the water, about ten feet above Helina. They were closing in on her fast, even through the force of the whirlpool.

"Pull back!" Mona screamed down at the men. But it was too late. They reached the squid and began attacking it in the water, even as they continued to swirl around and around. "No! They shouldn't be attacking it! It will only strengthen its grip around her. Corrine and Ibrahim, keep up the whirlpool while I go down there."

She began drifting downward into the eye of the swirling mass of water. A burst of white-blue fire shot from her palms, aimed directly at the squid's giant head. It took about ten bouts of fire from Mona before it finally exploded. Bright red liquid stained the water, and finally Helina was free from the tentacle.

Mona swooped down and lifted up Helina from the waves. She rushed up to us and laid her down on the rock before returning for the three men. We gathered over Helina. Her face scrunched up in pain, she was gripping her abdomen. Blood soaked her hands—at first I thought it might just be the squid's blood, but as Corrine bent down and loosened Helina's hands around her waist, there was a nasty-looking gash near her navel.

"I would rather use magic to heal this," Corrine said, looking at her husband. "It will be faster than waiting for Helina's natural healing capabilities to kick in. This is a deep gash."

Ibrahim bent down next to her and they began working on healing the vampire. Mona appeared on the rocks moments later with Erik, Matteo, and Kiev.

"Is she okay?" Matteo panted.

"She will be okay," Corrine said. "Just... don't come too close. We need space."

Silence fell among us as we stared down at the waters. The waves were settling and the corpse of the giant squid had bobbed up to the surface.

"Well, I'm sure we've attracted the merpeople's attention now," Mona said, her forehead creased with worry. "Just not the type of attention we want..."

CHAPTER 7: ROSE

"What do you mean?" my father asked Mona.

"We just killed one of their pets," the witch replied. "We came here to get information about Magnus. The odds of getting that from them were slim to start with… Now, I'm debating whether we should just leave. I have a bad feeling about staying in this place even a minute longer."

"We can't just leave," my mother replied. "That would be giving up. The Cove is the only thread we have to cling to."

Mona looked toward Matteo. "What are your thoughts?"

Matteo didn't look any less worried than Mona. He shrugged. "I'm not sure we have a choice but to take this risk. As Sofia said, if we leave now, then what?"

Mona gulped as all eyes turned to her again.

"Okay." She walked back over to the edge of the islet. The corpse of the squid was still floating above the waves, lapping against the rocks. Outstretching her palms, she uttered a spell. The monster's body vanished in an instant. "Let's hope nobody witnessed what just happened."

We gathered around the witches and traveled to the next islet.

"We should get down on the ground this time," my father said. "It will make it harder for squids to take aim at us."

Despite the crabs, I got down on all fours along with the others. Crawling to the edge and looking down at the water, I was surprised to see that it was tinged with a darker reddish color. "The squid's ink," Caleb said, following my gaze. "It's spread through the waves."

Great.

I almost leapt out of my skin as a high-pitched screech pierced the air. Mona swore beneath her breath. "Gather around," she hissed. "We've got to move to a different area."

I hurried toward Mona. Just before we vanished, I was able to catch sight of the source of the noise. Shooting out from the ocean fifty feet away, seated atop a giant horned seahorse, was a creature unlike any I had seen before. Half woman, half fish, she had skin consisting of green scales. She had a head of thick purplish hair, and her tail was long and slimy. Baring her teeth, she revealed a sharp set of black fangs.

Wow.

That is no Little Mermaid.

My heart was pounding in my chest as we reappeared in a different location. I could no longer hear the screeching and there was no tint of red in the ocean nearby, so I could only assume that Mona had taken us far away.

"Okay," Mona said, wiping sweat from her brow. "They know. It's only a matter of time before word spreads. We *must* find someone to speak to before that happens. I'm going to go down and try to find someone myself," she said, even as she looked terrified at the notion.

Kiev gripped her arm. "You said we couldn't enter the water without their permission."

"We don't have a choice now."

"Then you are not going alone," he said. "I for one will come with you."

"No, Kiev. One person entering is bad enough, two people will just get their guard up even more. I will go alone. Meanwhile, Corrine and Ibrahim will stay with you."

"But Mona," Ibrahim said, looking concerned. "What if we need to move? How will you find us?"

"We will find each other." Mona cast her eyes around at

the archipelago. "I will shoot up a flare once I am ready. If you detect any merfolk or other creature drawing close, vanish everyone a mile or so away from here. I will try to be back as fast as possible."

"I don't like this," Kiev said. He was still holding on to his wife.

"Neither do I," she replied, a pained expression on her face. "But we have no choice."

She shook herself free from Kiev and, without delaying a moment longer, dove into the water. I supposed that she would cast a spell on herself to allow her to survive beneath water.

The silence was chilling as Mona disappeared. We all looked at each other. Kiev had an agitated expression on his face.

"Let's keep to the center of this rock," my mother said, "as far away from the edges as possible."

"Just three of us should remain by the edges to check for anyone approaching," my father said. "I will keep guard. Who else would like to volunteer?"

He was deliberately avoiding looking toward my direction, but I called his attention, and Caleb followed me.

My father rolled his eyes. "You and Caleb can watch one corner, together."

"You think I would be able to sit while my wife is down there?" Kiev scowled. "I'll watch the third corner."

My mother joined my father on the side opposite us.

Caleb and I got down flat against the rocks and crawled to the edge, navigating past the crabs as best as we could. We lay on our stomachs and watched the gentle waves. A light breeze blew over us, causing goosebumps to run along my skin. The quiet was eerie. I could hear an occasional strange noise in the distance, but otherwise my ears were filled with nothing but the muttering of someone in our group and the lapping of the waves. I would have admired the beauty of this place were it not filled with such horrors.

Caleb reached for my hand and enveloped it.

"If something happens, promise me you won't do anything stupid," he said.

"Define stupid," I replied.

"You should be an expert at that definition by now."

I poked him in the shoulder.

"I define it as putting your life at risk," he said.

"I'll try not to. I mean, I *would* like to be alive for our wedding."

Caleb rolled his eyes.

I guessed that I wouldn't be of much use in this environment anyway. Unless a creature actually shot out of the water and I managed to aim my fire before it fell back in, the water would extinguish my flames. The most I could do, it seemed, was help keep watch.

"Rose! Caleb!" Micah shouted from behind us. "Watch

out!"

I whirled around to see a fat black-striped snake slithering toward us along the rocks. Caleb gripped my waist and jerked me backward away from it.

My breathing steadied as the snake made no motion to attack. It continued along its path, apparently uninterested in us. We waited until it had passed by and slithered downward, back toward the sea.

"And we are the ones who are supposed to be keeping watch…" I muttered.

We got down on all fours again and crawled back to our spot, resting on our stomachs.

"I was distracting us," Caleb said.

We spent what felt like the next hour in silence. There was still no sign of Mona.

"Something has happened," Kiev said. "I'm going down to look for her."

"You might end up causing more trouble than good," Matteo said. "If she's in the middle of some kind of negotiation, your presence might mess it up… Mona is powerful enough to look after herself."

Kiev scowled. "I'll wait half an hour more. Then, Corrine and Ibrahim, I will need you to cast the same spell on me that Mona put on herself."

Kiev's nerves were getting to me. I was beginning to imagine the worst. Even though I knew Mona was a powerful witch, we had no idea what was within the depths of this ocean.

Half an hour passed quickly and then Kiev approached the witch and warlock. "I just want to find Mona. If I see she is in the middle of a conversation, obviously I won't step in. I just want to locate her and know that she is safe."

Corrine and Ibrahim looked reluctant, but they gave in to Kiev's request. Once Ibrahim had finished casting a spell on him, Kiev removed his shirt, revealing his prosthetic arm, and dove headfirst into the murky waters. I shivered watching him disappear.

"I hope that wasn't a mistake," Matteo muttered.

Somehow, I couldn't help but feel that it was. Although I understood how Kiev felt. I would have reacted the same.

A screech echoed around the rocks. It sounded much closer than any I had heard in the past hour and a half. Too close. I looked back toward my parents. They too looked alarmed.

Now we had both Kiev and Mona beneath the water. If we left, it would be relatively easy for Mona to locate us, but what if Kiev didn't manage to find Mona and surfaced looking for us? How would he find us again?

"Over there," Aiden whispered, horror in his eyes.

I followed the direction he was pointing toward and gasped. Through a thick film of sea spray, I could make out dozens of merfolk—male and female—seated atop the same giant seahorses as the one I had seen earlier and carrying long, razor-sharp spears. They shot out of the water, reaching high into the sky—high enough to see above the islets. If I had thought the previous screech was loud, now the noise had intensified tenfold. They all screeched at once, racing toward us at an alarming speed.

My father had seconds to decide what we were to do. Stay here and try to head them off, or flee and risk Kiev being lost.

"Ibrahim. Corrine. Put up a shield. Now!"

Caleb caught my hand and pulled me farther toward the center as the warlock and witch secured the islet.

Sweat was dripping from Corrine's forehead. "Neither Ibrahim nor I have encountered creatures like this before," she said. "We have to hope our shield will keep them out."

We all backed close to each other in the center of the rocks, watching as the creatures came within thirty feet, twenty feet, ten feet…

We braced ourselves as they shot straight toward our islet. Ten soared through the air on their fierce-looking seahorses, but to my relief, they hit against the barrier and slid back into the ocean. My father walked closer to the barrier as more began hitting up against it. The merpeople let out angry hisses, revealing long snakelike tongues. Matteo approached behind my father.

"We are not here to harm you," Matteo said. "We have

come to ask some simple questions and then we will leave."

I wondered if the merpeople could even understand what Matteo was saying. They continued to hiss and glare up at us as they bobbed in the waves.

The three closest to the front exchanged glances. The looks on their faces told me that they were open to anything but to talking now.

My heart pounded as several of them leapt up toward us again, their spears aimed directly at the barrier. I took a step back involuntarily. Thankfully, the barrier held up, or a number of us would have likely found ourselves with holes through our chests.

They slipped back down, and then to my surprise, dipped beneath the waves and disappeared.

I hadn't been expecting them to disappear so quickly. From the look on everyone's faces, nobody had been. But the fact that we knew for sure that so many were now in this area—so close to where Mona and Kiev had disappeared—was worrying. Especially if they caught Kiev on his own. He only had one arm.

"What now?" I asked.

"We wait some more," my father replied. "We shouldn't leave the spot now until they have returned."

I hated to voice such a question, but I couldn't help myself. "What if they don't return?"

My father shot me a sharp glance. "Let's just take this

one hour at a time."

I was about to take a seat back down on the rocks when a chilling sight arrested me. A wave was rolling toward us in the distance. A towering, monstrous wave.

"What the—"

My spine tingled as it seemed to be picking up speed, now only three islets away from us.

"Uh, Corrine," my mother said, her voice trembling, "This barrier should be strong enough to withstand water, right?"

Corrine and Ibrahim's mouths hung open as they stared at the wall of water.

"Water, yes…. B-But that?" Corrine gasped as she pointed toward the base of the wave.

Now that it was nearer, I realized what she had spotted. The base of the wave was oddly discolored compared to the rest. There was a dark brown shadow.

"Oh my God," I rasped. "It's a… creature."

Barely had I said the words when a set of jagged jaws the diameter of eight grown men poked through the wall of water, followed by two slanted pitch-black eyes. A spiky fin ran from the top of its head down along its spine and stopped at the end of its gargantuan tail. The only way I could think to describe it was as some kind of prehistoric sea monster. Or Frankenstein's piranha.

Hurtling straight toward us, it smashed headfirst into

the rocks. There was a deafening crack as the base of the islet shattered beneath the sheer force of the monstrous creature. The ground beneath us disintegrated, the ocean gushing up and consuming us. Sucked down into the water, I feared that the suction of the sinking islet would hold me under long after my lungs gave way. I splashed about, having no idea where Caleb was, or any of my family and friends. For all I knew, I could have been floating inches away from some kind of dreadful creature, perhaps the sea monster itself.

Relief washed over me as a strong warm hand gripped my arm. I didn't need vision to know that it was my father. He pulled me upward until we reached the surface. I gasped for breath, wiping the water from my eyes.

"Where is everyone else?" I panted.

"We need to find them," he said.

"There's Corrine!" I pointed out at the sky to see a battered-looking Corrine hovering above us.

Before she could make it to us, a deep bellow rumbled through the water and vibrated through my insides. My father and I looked behind us in horror to see a mass of dark shadow beneath the water. An overwhelming suction pulled us downward and we were submerged once again in the ocean.

I opened my eyes underwater even though it stung. Ten feet away from us were the gaping jaws of the sea monster.

It was sucking us toward it. Even my father was helpless against its strength. In a last-ditch attempt, my father and I tried to summon our fire powers—it was useless, of course. Like trying to light a wet match.

No.

Just as the monster's teeth were a few feet away from closing down around us, a sudden weight from above hit hard against my shoulders. I found myself being dragged down further into the sea, narrowly missing being gouged by the monster's lower set of serrated teeth. My father was pulled down too next to me. I looked down to see that it was Corrine. She had grabbed both of our ankles and was yanking us down, out of direct aim of the monster.

Caleb hurtled toward the head of the creature. His right leg was covered in blood and his chest marred with cuts. He held one of the merfolk's spears in his right hand. I opened my mouth to scream as he made contact with the creature's skull. Balancing himself above it, he drove the spear through the roof of the monster's mouth. A deafening bellow filled the ocean as it thrashed violently. Its movement sent Corrine, my father and me hurtling further down into the depths of the sea.

I couldn't even see what had happened to Caleb. Corrine gripped my and my father's arms and propelled us upward with speed that would have been impossible without magic. I looked down to see the blood spilling from the monster's head as it retreated further into darkness.

But where is Caleb?

"Caleb!" I screamed, as we hit the surface. I looked around wildly. "Caleb!"

"I'm here," a strained voice called. Caleb had just resurfaced a few meters away from us. Despite his injuries, he swam toward us quickly. Corrine then magicked us all to a nearby rock where other members of our group were waiting, many of them injured. I barely had a chance to look around before Ibrahim and Corrine began ushering us all together in a circle and we vanished.

We reappeared again on another islet—quiet, with no signs of the destruction we had just left. We all looked battle-worn—clearly many of us had attempted to battle the mermaids, judging by the various gashes in our bodies. My eyes traveled from Aiden, to Ashley, Landis, Helina, Erik, Ibrahim, Corrine, Micah, Caleb, my father, Matteo… But no matter how many times I looked around, I couldn't see my mother.

My father's eyes lit up with panic as he realized the same thing.

"Where is Sofia?" He leapt to his feet and gripped Ibrahim's shoulders.

"What?" Ibrahim choked. He and Corrine cast their eyes around disbelievingly.

"How could we have missed her?" Corrine gasped.

CHAPTER 8: SOFIA

As I fought to the surface, a slimy hand closed around my ankle.

I was yanked painfully downward, managing to take one last deep breath before my head submerged. I opened my eyes in the murky water and could just about make out the outline of a merman through the weeds. I kicked with all my strength, but his hold on me remained. I tried to bend down to lash out with my claws. He let go of me to dodge, but then another merman approached behind me. He caught my arms and pinned them behind my back.

No.

The first merman reached for my ankle again and the two of them dragged me down. I squirmed and continued to fight, but I couldn't break free from their grasp. I looked up at the rapidly disappearing surface. As a vampire, I could hold my breath much longer than a human... but not forever.

As we descended deeper and deeper, the weeds grew thinner, the murkiness lifting and the water becoming clearer. My eyes widened at the sight that was now beneath me. I had a bird's eye view of a magnificent underwater city. Paths lined with coral formed a maze around stone buildings. Gardens of sea flora and forests of tall sea grass were scattered between the constructions.

I was expecting the mermen to begin dragging me down toward the buildings, but to my surprise, they didn't. They stopped descending and continued swimming with me at this level, past monstrous black sharks, luminous blue jellyfish the size of cars, pure white dolphins, and other alien creatures. We weaved in and out of the bases of the islets that served as majestic columns for the city. I wanted to scream out to them to let me go, but opening my mouth would only hasten my demise. I couldn't afford to start swallowing water.

We started approaching one of the columns and they began swimming upward again. As they drifted with me higher and higher, I hoped for a moment that they were about to take me back up to the surface, but they stopped about fifteen feet beneath the surface. They swam right up to the rocks and now I could make out a dark hole. They pulled me through it, traveling along a narrow tunnel that had apparently been drilled right through the base of this islet, and I was brought an unexpected reprieve. My head popped above water, sweet oxygen filling my lungs. I gasped, looking around. We were in a cave. They hauled me out of the water and pinned me down against the rough ground.

They tied some kind of rope tightly around my ankles and arms. They were hog-tying me. They rolled me onto my side where I could better make out the cave. It was empty except for two still forms lying in the corner. As the stinging in my eyes from the salt water subsided, and my vision returned, I realized that it was Kiev and Mona—unconscious.

"What do you want with us?" I gasped at the two mermen.

They just shoved me farther away from the entrance to the cave and then disappeared back into the water.

"No," I groaned in despair. I looked back at Mona and Kiev. "Mona? Kiev?"

No answer. They didn't budge an inch.

Fear gripped me as I wondered if they were even still alive. They appeared to be tied up, like me, and that was the only comfort I had, for I could not see them breathing.

I lost track of how long I lay there. I had no idea what

I'd been captured for, or what they were going to do with me. The wait was agonizing. I found myself wondering if anyone was going to come at all, or whether they just intended to leave me—us—here to rot. I looked across the floor at the pool. I even considered dipping back into the water. But that would be suicide. Whatever they had tied around me was incredibly strong and I couldn't break free no matter how much I fought.

My head was beginning to feel light—perhaps from shock—and my eyelids were growing heavy. Although I was glad for the oxygen, it didn't feel like there was much of it in here. It also felt humid and hot. I felt claustrophobic, despite the highness of the ceiling above me.

My eyes shot toward the entrance of the cave as I heard a splash. Green scaly hands gripped the sides of the hole and a mermaid with flaming orange hair and a pearl-studded tiara emerged.

"Please," I said, before she could have a chance to do anything to me. "You must understand why we are here. We don't mean to cause harm. We are—"

"I already know what you claim to be here for." Her voice was much softer to the ear than I'd expected. It was smooth, almost melodious. Quite a contradiction to the screeching sound I was used to these creatures making. A smile formed on her thin lips. "It is insulting that you expect us to believe such a story. Don't you think you have insulted us enough already by murdering one of our wardens?"

"It is the truth," I said, as calmly as I could. "We've come here in search of a vampire named Magnus because we wish to end the black witches. You must help us. If you don't, even your own realm could be at risk from them."

"Enough," she said, anger now sparking in her eyes. "I know that you are allied with the black witches. I won't tell you where Magnus is, so I suggest you forget about that. I will, however, make sure the last hours of your life are as uncomfortable as possible."

With that, she turned her back to me and slithered along the floor toward a raised platform in one corner that looked over the entire cave.

She reached down to the ground and picked up what looked like a thin tube. Placing it between her lips, she turned to face me directly and blew out in one sharp breath. The next thing I knew, something dug into my shoulder, and then a heat burned and spread through my shoulder to my neck, my chest, until my whole body was stinging. My vision shrouded and after a minute, all went black.

Chapter 9: Rose

Corrine and Ibrahim vanished and went back to check for my mother. When they returned unsuccessful, my father, grandfather and I were panicking.

"Take me back there," my father demanded.

He stood next to Ibrahim. Before he could vanish, I hurried over to him and so did my grandfather. When Caleb approached too, I turned to him. "You don't need to come," I said.

"If you're going, I'm coming with you."

And so we all vanished and reappeared back in the area where the monster had smashed into the islet. There were no living creatures around now, from what I could see.

"Allow us to breathe underwater," my father said,

addressing the warlock and witch. "And also make us invisible."

"We need a plan, Derek," Aiden said. "If we are all invisible, how are we going to communicate with each other? How will we prevent ourselves from getting lost?"

"We should be tied together," Caleb said.

"Yes," Ibrahim said. He and Corrine went about casting the first spell over us—I couldn't feel any difference once they had finished, but I assumed that I would feel it once I dove into the water. "Now," Ibrahim continued, "if I am to tie everyone together, we need to decide in what order we are going to be swimming. Who will go in front?"

My father was already ordering us all into a line. He suggested that Aiden go at the back, then Caleb, me, Corrine, Ibrahim, and himself at the front. Standing in this order, I felt something thick wrap around my waist and tighten. It felt like a rope, though it wasn't visible to the eye.

Next, the warlock and witch made us all invisible. I reached behind me and felt for Caleb's hand. I squeezed it tight.

"This invisibility won't help us much," my father said. "We'll still be disturbing the water currents and producing a scent and taste in the water. So we need to move as fast as we possibly can."

My father tugged us all forward and we dove into the

ocean. I trusted that Ibrahim and Corrine's breathing spell had worked—and indeed it had. It was the strangest thing. I no longer felt the need to inhale. It wasn't a strain keeping my mouth closed because I felt no desire to open it. I wondered how long a spell like this could last on a human body. Hopefully long enough.

I also wondered if Mona had placed this invisibility spell on herself when she had entered the ocean. Kiev should've had it done to him too. He hadn't even given Corrine or Ibrahim the chance to suggest it; he had been in such a hurry to go after Mona.

As we swam deeper and deeper through the dark green weeds, Caleb's hands rested at my sides. I was still terrified of what we were about to encounter, but his touch brought me at least some reassurance.

The water became less murky as we descended deeper, and soon all the weeds had disappeared. I could barely believe my eyes at what I saw beneath me... a stunning underwater kingdom.

My father stopped swimming, causing all of us to pause. I assumed that he was looking around and deciding in which direction we ought to head first.

It wasn't long before he started moving again, guiding us all downward after him. My skin crawled at all the creatures that were now in full view. Creatures of my nightmares. Giant sharks, water serpents, more bright red squid, more crabs—much larger than those we had seen on the rocks—and bizarre-looking fish that came in various shapes and sizes. The only thing they all had in common was that none of them looked friendly.

I was petrified that we might collide with one of the creatures head-on. Especially at the speed my father had begun to drag us downward. He didn't seem to be concerned at all by what we were passing by. Apparently, we were heading directly for the entrance to the kingdom. As we neared it, a merman came into view. He held a tall spear and was prowling around near the pearl-studded entrance gates.

I wanted to ask what on earth my father was thinking as he hurtled so close to him. But before I could, the merman's spear shot right out of his hand and vanished—I could only assume beneath my father's touch. The merman looked shocked as he stared around. Then the man vanished too.

Oh my God. My father is taking him hostage.

I just hoped that this would not end in disaster.

"Where do you keep your prisoners?" My father's voice drifted through the water.

There was much hissing and protesting on the part of the merman, but it seemed that my father was not letting up.

"Tell me," he growled. "And I might just spare your

life."

I could hear the sound of a struggle and we were all pulled forward and backward several times before my father finally overpowered the creature.

"All right," the creature gasped. "I will lead you."

"And no *mis*leading me," my father said, his voice nothing short of menacing. "This spear will be lodged deep into your throat if I detect even the slightest bit of deceit from you."

To my surprise, we headed upward. I was expecting us to enter the city. We began traveling at a much faster speed—I guessed that the merman was doing much of the work in pulling us forward with his powerful tail.

The base of an islet came into view. Swimming up to it, the merman led us through a hole that was drilled right through its base. He led us into it. Traveling along a dark tunnel, we surfaced in a pool in the center of a dark cave. We hauled ourselves out of the water. It was empty but for three figures lying on the ground. Mona and Kiev were lying in one corner, while my mother was in another. I lurched toward her and clutched her face. It shook me to see how she'd been tied up. Like an animal. I pressed my ear against her chest, afraid that I might not even hear a heartbeat. But I did, however faint it was. The rope Ibrahim and Corrine had connected us with tugged around my waist as others must have been walking toward the other end of the cave.

"Loosen the rope," my father said, his voice some distance away. For a moment, I wondered why he hadn't immediately rushed over to my mother. But then I remembered that he was still restraining the merman.

The rope around me loosened.

"Gather them up quickly," my father said. "We don't have long."

I felt Caleb next to me as I slid my hands beneath my mother's body. He placed his hands beneath her legs and we both stood up, lifting her up with us. But as we motioned to move back toward the entrance of the cave, something held us in place.

"They have fastened her to the ground," Caleb said.

A chain had been locked around my mother's right arm. We were forced to put her back down. The chain clanged as Caleb attacked it, but it seemed that he was having trouble loosening it from the ground.

"Corrine," he called across the cave. "Are Kiev and Mona fastened to the ground?"

"Yes," Corrine replied, her voice filled with worry. "Ibrahim and I are trying to break the chains. They are made of—"

My father grunted, then yelled out, "No!"

The merman he had taken hostage came into view. He had broken free from my father's grasp and dove into the water.

"Hurry," my father said, now rushing over to us. "He slipped from my grasp. We need to get out of here, now!"

"I don't know what these chains are made of," Ibrahim said. "It's stronger than any material I've ever encountered. We're trying to break them."

My father attacked the chain connected to my mother, but he had no more luck than Caleb had.

"I wonder if burning it might help?" I suggested.

"Pick her up again," my father said.

Caleb and I did as he had requested. A moment later, a blaze of fire scorched the ground where the chain was connected. It still remained fixed.

"We figured it out!" Ibrahim called. We turned to see him carrying Mona in his arms, free from any chains.

Corrine hurried over to us and Ibrahim started to work on Kiev's chain.

"All right, hurry," my father said.

My heart leapt into my throat as a hissing sound filled the cave. Five mermen surfaced in the pool and hauled themselves up onto the ground.

They all carried two spears, one in each hand, and they looked more fierce than I had ever seen these creatures looking before. My mother still being attached to the ground, Caleb and I crouched down on the ground with her, keeping contact with her so that she remained invisible. The mermen must have been warned that we were invisible foes. Spears outstretched, they began whirling them around wildly.

Oh, Lord.

I crawled over my mother and lay down against her as flat as I could as one merman headed straight for us. One of his blades grazed the air, inches above my ear. I gasped, fearing that he was about to strike again. Instead he yelled and staggered backward. Two nasty gashes appeared across his face—claw marks. I heard Caleb's heavy breathing as the merman lashed out again with both spears.

"Make everyone visible!" my father bellowed somewhere across the cave.

"No!" I cried. I couldn't understand why my father would order that. But my protest went in vain. I became visible, as did every other person in the cave. It was then that I caught sight of Caleb standing several feet away from me, blood soaking his claws.

The mermen launched forward now with confidence.

My father's purpose for such an insane order finally became clear to me as he yelled, "Duck!"

He wanted everyone in sight so he could be sure he wasn't about to scorch anyone.

Although they looked confused, everyone obeyed his commands and billows of fire shot from his palms toward the two mermen nearest him. A wave of heat hit my face.

The creatures screeched and staggered back as the flames engulfed them. They launched toward the exit of the cave and dove into the water to extinguish themselves.

The merman closest to me had spotted my mother and me on the ground. He motioned to move toward us. I shot to my feet and released a burst of fire. I was surprised at how quickly it sprung from my palms. His eyes widened in shock, and he hurried backward, but he wasn't fast enough to escape my fire. As with the other two my father had targeted, he dove screeching into the water to extinguish himself. Only two mermen remained in the chamber now. They were harassing Matteo and Caleb.

"Duck!" my father and I yelled at once.

The mermen already knew what was coming. They didn't wait around and moved their slimy bodies straight for the pool. Our flames only licked their tails.

My father then walked over to the entrance of the cave and remained standing over it, positioning his palms above the water threateningly in case any of them got the idea to come back in. The moment they raised their heads out of the water, they would be burnt to a crisp.

Now that the mermen were out of the way, Corrine raced back over to my mother. She managed to detach the chain from her, allowing me to finally pick my mother up with the help of Caleb and carry her toward my father. Ibrahim brought Mona, while Erik carried Kiev's unconscious form over to us. Once everyone had gathered round, and we had done a headcount just to be sure we hadn't left anyone behind this time, my father turned to Corrine and Ibrahim.

"Take everyone to safety now."

"What?" I said, gaping at him. "You're coming too."

He shook his head and glared at Corrine.

The witch gripped my arm and my father, along with the cave, disappeared from sight.

***

As we were reunited with the rest of our group on the rocks, Caleb and I laid my mother down gently. I leapt up and clutched Ibrahim's arm. "Why did we leave my father?"

"Don't worry," he said. "I'm going back to get him."

"But why did we leave him?"

Corrine placed a gentle hand over my shoulder. "He's going to try to get the information we need about Magnus. Without that, our entire trip will have been a waste."

"How will he get that information?"

"Just… Have some faith in your father, Rose," Ibrahim said, and a moment later, he had vanished again.

Blood still pounding in my ears, I made my way back over to my mother and placed a hand over her head. Then I bent over and kissed her cold cheeks.

Corrine approached beside me and began examining her. She reached for my mother's ripped shirt and pulled it down so that the skin of her shoulders was revealed. The witch ran a finger over a bright red spot. At least, I had thought it was a spot. She bent down closer and, after a moment of fiddling, pulled out a small bullet-shaped object from my mother's flesh.

"A poison dart," Corrine said, sniffing it.

"Poison?" I said, horrified.

"Yes, but it's not lethal." She gestured toward the other side of the rock. "Why don't you sit over there while I treat your mother? I have my own nerves to contend with without yours too."

I didn't want to leave, but I figured that Corrine would work better without me there, so I did.

I approached Caleb, who was sitting on the ground, nursing his injured leg. He had ripped the bottom half of his trousers off to reveal a deep cut just beneath his shin. It was so deep, I thought I could almost see bone.

"Why isn't it healing?" I said worriedly, bending down.

"It will," he said through gritted teeth. "I think those spears are tinged with something that makes the healing process slower."

My eyes fell to his chest. That seemed to be healing a bit better than his leg. I gripped his head, winding my fingers into his hair and pressing my lips against his, kissing him passionately. I pulled away, staring into his eyes.

"Sometimes stupid pays off."

He let out a weak chuckle. "Sometimes."

"Let's just hope it pays off for my father…"

I walked to the edge of the rocks we were standing on and looked down at the water.

Come on, Ibrahim, what's taking you so long?

I heaved a huge sigh of relief when the two men finally appeared on the island. My father had more cuts than when I had last seen him, but he seemed to be all right. I hurried up to him and flung myself into his arms.

"What happened?" I asked.

He looked around at everyone grimly. "I waited in a corner to trick the mermen into believing that we had all gone. As soon as they pulled themselves up out of the water, I managed to grab hold of one and coerce him into speaking to me. The long and the short of it is, Magnus is no longer here in The Cove."

Everyone's faces dropped.

Oh, man.

"Then where is he?" Aiden asked.

"The merman didn't seem sure of the vampire's whereabouts," my father replied. "Apparently he hasn't been seen in these parts for at least a century. The merman advised to try searching for him in The Woodlands. I wasn't able to stay long enough for him to explain what

The Woodlands is. Does anybody know?"

"The werewolf realm," Micah said instantly.

We all eyed one another.

"Well," Ashley muttered, scowling as she stood next to Landis and nursed a wounded elbow, "looks like this has officially become a goose chase."

Chapter 10: Rhys

We took Lilith's unconscious form up to a bedroom. Isolde and Julisse bathed her, then laid her down on a bed. We all looked on as she breathed gently, her eyelids still shut. It was bizarre seeing Lilith in this youthful form. I was so used to seeing her as a corpse. Of course, she wouldn't remain like this forever. But it would be long enough to complete the final part of the ritual.

"Aunt," I said, "would you step out of the room with me for a moment?"

Isolde looked confused at my request, but she turned to Julisse and said, "Stay here with Lilith."

I led my aunt out of the bedroom and along the corridor outside until we were well out of earshot.

"What is it?" she asked.

"About the final step," I said, bracing myself for her reaction. "Our plan needs to be modified slightly."

"What do you mean?"

"I mean that I have a way to make the ritual less prone to failure. We both know how fragile Lilith's existence is, even in her young form. It's possible she won't make it through to the end—and that is a possibility that we can't afford to entertain. The bond she had with Magnus... it has been enough to sustain her until now, but this ritual will put levels of stress on her that she has never had to bear before." I paused, studying my aunt's face for a moment before continuing. "Isolde, I went against Lilith's wishes."

"What?" she whispered.

"I imprisoned Magnus."

My aunt's jaw dropped. "What? How?"

"When we first came into contact with Lilith and I learned about her secret, I confronted her about Magnus. I told her that we couldn't afford for anything to happen to him. Even as a vampire, he was and is not invulnerable. I knew that we needed to keep him alive for a long time. Anything could happen to him before we were ready to carry out the ritual. But Lilith refused to even entertain my suggestion. She wouldn't tell me why, she just rejected it outright. She said that nothing would happen to him and imprisoning him wasn't necessary. I tried to press at the time, tried to make her see reason, but she wouldn't hear me out." I shot a look down the corridor to check that we were still alone. "So I took matters into my own hands. I tracked the vampire down and placed him somewhere… secure."

My aunt looked dumbstruck. "All this time," she breathed, "you never told me. Why?"

"I didn't tell anybody," I said. "Not even my sisters. There was no point until we were ready to call upon him. I didn't want to worry you. You had enough on your shoulders already."

"But… We can't just bring him in front of Lilith. If she finds out about your deception, your disobedience, she will be furious. God knows what she might do."

I gripped my aunt's arm and led her further along the corridor, lowering my voice even more. "She will thank me for it. It will be a shock, no doubt about that. But having Magnus present with her in the flesh will make the bond she has with him as strong as it can possibly be."

"All this is just your speculation. You have no idea how she will react."

I breathed out impatiently. "We won't reveal Magnus until the ritual has started. Do you really think that she would interrupt it?"

Isolde still looked doubtful.

"Look," I said. "This is just a risk we have to take. And I

need you on my side."

She swallowed hard, then said, "All right. Where have you kept the vampire?"

"I will explain later," I said. "Now, while Lilith is still recovering, I am going to fetch him and bring him back to the castle. We'll keep him locked in a room until we are ready to begin."

"I hope you are sure about this, Rhys."

I nodded. "In the end, Lilith will thank me for it. As will generations of witches in the future."

Chapter 11: Rhys

I looked around the silent wood. It had been a while since I had last been here. Still, I knew exactly where to go. I launched into a sprint, whipping through the trees until they thinned and gave way to the foot of a large gray mountain. I had chosen this spot specifically because it was one of the least densely populated areas of the werewolf realm. I began my climb and stopped halfway up.

I pulled myself up on to a ledge and stared directly ahead of me at the rocky wall. To all appearances, this wall looked no different from the rest of the mountain. There were also plenty of ridges like the one I was standing on. The small octagonal mark inscribed in the center of the wall assured me that this was the right one.

I walked up and placed my palms against it. I pressed my right ear against the cool stone and listened. Then, when I uttered a charm, the wall gave way, swinging backward. Dust and small rocks loosened and fell on me as I stepped into a small cave. It was dark and musty—empty but for a long casket lining one wall. Manifesting a flame in my palm to shed light, I headed for the stone container. It was freezing cold to the touch—as it should be. Loosening the two clasps that held down the lid, I pulled it open.

My eyes widened, my mouth drying out.

It was empty.

What?

I looked around the cave again, half expecting to see the vampire stepping out from the shadows. Confusion fogged my brain.

Where is he?

How on earth could he have escaped?

There was no sign of any efforts to break out of this cave, and there were no holes or crannies that he could have escaped through. Besides, I had put him to sleep. How would he have even woken up?

None of it made any sense.

I could only assume that I had been careless in casting my spell upon him, and somehow he had gotten the wall to open. I had been a more inexperienced warlock at that time, after all. I had not yet undergone the sacrifices that had shaped my powers into what they were today.

Sweat formed on my forehead. Lilith was waiting for me to return before starting the ritual. I couldn't keep her waiting much longer. I had to find this vampire.

At least I knew the first place that I needed to look.

If Magnus had indeed woken up and escaped, he would have been incredibly weak. It would have been a strain just to make it down the mountain. I couldn't believe that he would've left this realm without werewolves coming across him. They would have detected the scent of a vampire from miles away. At least I knew for sure that he was still alive, otherwise Lilith would be gone by now. I just had to find him.

I rushed back down the mountain and through the woods toward the nearest werewolf habitation. It was still early morning, and most likely they would all still be in their wolf forms. It didn't matter to me either way. I would get what I needed from them.

Approaching a more densely populated area, I could already smell wolf in the air. It wasn't long before one of the beasts came into view. It was a mother and cub, bathing in a nearby stream. I remained within the shadows, drawing nearer and nearer. I had made sure to cover up my scent with a charm before I even entered this island.

By the time the mother noticed me, it was already too late. Brushing the cub aside, I leapt onto her back, wrapping my arms around her throat and bringing her into submission.

She thrashed beneath me, but I only closed down on her windpipe harder, until she couldn't breathe at all.

"Listen carefully to me, dog," I hissed into her ear. "If you ever want to see your child again, you will take me to your chieftain."

"Run!" she choked to her cub.

The small wolf, his eyes lit with panic, began scampering away. Still holding onto his mother, I summoned him back toward me.

"Don't mess with me," I said, my voice soft and dangerous. "Take me to your chieftain now."

CHAPTER 12: ROSE

Before attempting to enter the realm of the werewolves, we headed back to the Tavern. Ibrahim and Corrine made us appear back on the beach, outside the walls lining the island. We hadn't stayed long enough in The Cove for my mother, Kiev and Mona to recover. But now that we were out of danger, we laid them all down on the beach where Ibrahim and Corrine could work on them without worrying about another attack.

Our first priority was bringing them to consciousness before treating those who had been wounded during the fight. Now that Corrine and Ibrahim had removed the poison darts from their flesh, the process was faster. After only a quarter of an hour, my mother finally sat up. I wanted to leap at her, but I held myself back. Her eyelids were half closed as she looked around, frowning and looking bewildered. Her dry lips parted.

"Mom," I said.

Her eyes fixed on me, widening.

"Rose," she croaked.

She attempted to get to her feet, but her legs were still shaky. My father picked her up in his arms and kissed her.

"You're safe now," he said. I walked over to them. My mother reached down and touched my face, then pulled me closer so that she could kiss my forehead.

Kiev and Mona were now waking up too—both looking just as confused as my mother.

"Wh-Where am I?" Mona stuttered.

"You've just woken from a stupor induced by poison darts," Corrine explained.

Kiev groaned, clutching his head.

Now that all three were clearly all right, I moved back over to Caleb sitting on the sand. Most of his cuts had closed up by now, but the gash in his leg was still having trouble healing. Corrine and Ibrahim were moving from person to person, and I was relieved when Corrine reached Caleb. It wasn't long before his leg was patched up and he could stand normally. He headed straight for the ocean and dipped into the waves, cleaning off the bloodstains. Realizing that I too could use a wash, I joined him.

Everyone else soon followed our lead. Once we were done refreshing ourselves as much as we could, we climbed out of the water and onto the sand.

Mona, Kiev and my mother had apparently already been filled in on what had happened since they'd lost consciousness.

"So," my mother said, looking nervous, "we head to the Woodlands now?"

Mona nodded. "Hopefully Magnus' trail will be hotter there."

"You will need to make me invisible and also hide my scent," Micah said.

"Why?" Ibrahim asked.

"Because I'm not welcome there."

"What did you do?" I asked, raising a brow. I recalled the story that Rhys had told me about Micah—how he had been banished for falling in love with a chieftain's daughter while she was betrothed to another. I wondered whether there was any truth in that at all.

"I clashed with the chieftain who ruled my pack. I didn't agree with many of the decisions he made, and I was vocal about it. He thought that it would be easier to get rid of me. So I was banished from his pack. I moved to another, then another, but I couldn't find a chieftain I could respect enough to submit to. In the end, I just left. I preferred a life of freedom."

"I see," Mona said. "Well, we will be sure to cover you up."

"We should leave now," my father said.

We gathered together and I braced myself for my stomach to lurch once again as we hurtled through the air at lightning speed.

When I opened my eyes, I was clutching Caleb tight. We were standing on a cluster of giant boulders, the waves lapping at our feet.

"Now would be a good time to disguise me," Micah said. "Someone might have sensed me already. I also suggest that you all do the same. Vampires and witches are anything but welcome here, while humans"—his eyes fell on my father and me—"are considered a delicacy by wolves."

Mona, Ibrahim and Corrine set about following Micah's suggestion.

Once Corrine had finished with Caleb and me, I looked down at my hands. They had disappeared. It wasn't long before everyone was invisible. I caught Caleb's hand.

"Now, Micah, where would you suggest we start?" my father asked.

"Hmm. Well, let's think," the werewolf replied. "Unless Magnus had the help of witches to cover his scent, I'm sure that the wolves would have detected the vampire's presence sooner or later. So if he stayed for a stretch of time, the wolves would have known about it. That brings two options. Either they caught him and threw him straight out—or perhaps murdered him—or they allowed him to stay. If we assume the second option, then Magnus would have needed permission from a chieftain."

"So we need to seek out chieftains?" Ashley asked.

"Yes," Micah replied.

"You can't sense any vampires now?" Aiden asked.

"I can only sense you guys," Micah replied. "It could be that we're not close enough to Magnus for me to sense him yet. The Woodlands is a massive place."

"So where do we go first?" Corrine asked.

"To the woods," Micah said.

My eyes traveled past the rocky shore we were standing on, and toward the dark forest that lined it. Although day was close to breaking, the trees were so thick, I was sure that it would be almost as dark walking beneath them as if it were night.

We hurried away from the rocks and approached the entrance to the woods.

"It's bizarre to be back here. It's been so long," Micah murmured.

We began walking along the winding forest path. The noises around us gave me chills—shrill chirping and the occasional grunting of an animal. Boughs creaked and the wind rustled the leaves of the trees.

Perhaps half an hour passed before it appeared that the trees were beginning to thin. I thought at first that it might just be my imagination, but then I could make out an opening in the distance. We reached it quickly and found ourselves stepping onto the edge of a cliff. The landscape before us took my breath away. The cliff dropped sharply downward toward a sea of trees and surrounding the area were endless mountain ranges. I realized that this place reminded me a little of The Shade, albeit on a much grander scale.

"Do you see that mountain far in the distance, directly in front of us?" Micah asked. "It's probably the tallest in sight."

There was a veil of mist in the distance, and since it wasn't even fully daylight yet, I struggled to see what Micah was pointing to.

"I see it," several vampires replied.

"That is where my pack used to live," Micah said.

"How many packs are there in this realm?" Caleb asked.

Micah scoffed. "Too many to count. The Woodlands is a divided realm—centuries of disagreements have caused much discord and separation."

"So how do we know which chieftain to approach?"

"We don't. But let's try here first. The shore we arrived on is the primary way into this realm," Micah said. "And this chieftain's territory spans—or at least used to span—

many miles from here, so if Magnus arrived, it's likely that he would have been detected by one of the werewolves of this chieftain's pack before he made it into another area."

"Okay," my father said.

"Ibrahim, Corrine and Mona," Micah said, "you can magick us there now."

We all felt our way toward each other, and disappeared once the witches were sure that everyone was touching. The temperature dropped sharply as we reappeared at the base of a mountain. It was only now that we were here that I realized the sheer scale of it. It made me dizzy just craning my head upward and trying to see the top. It was certainly taller than any skyscraper I had seen. The tip disappeared into the clouds.

I looked back behind us, trying to see where we had just been standing, and even now I could barely make it out through the fog.

"Now what?" I asked.

"I suggest that you and your father head up the mountain alone and try to get a meeting with the chieftain," Micah said.

"What?" my mother said, alarm in her voice. "But they are humans. I thought you said—"

"Of all of us, Rose and Derek will get these wolves' backs up the least. Humans are not intimidating to werewolves as vampires and witches are. Wolves are distrustful of intruders enough as it is. I think I can speak for all of us in saying that we don't want to cause another showdown here like we had in The Cove."

"But why does Rose need to come?" my father said. "I'll go alone. I can wield fire if something goes wrong. I will be able to manage even if a whole pack of wolves launches an attack on me. In any case"—he looked toward the brightening sky—"they will be in their human forms anytime now."

"Derek," Micah said, "you're an intimidating guy, to put it mildly. Having a young woman like Rose next to you will help to soften things a little."

"All right," my father said after a pause, reluctance in his tone. "So, Corrine, you will need to remove Rose's and my invisibility now."

"Also, Corrine, stop suppressing their scent," Micah said. "If the wolves can't smell them, that will also make them distrustful."

My father appeared before me, and then I became visible as well. I walked toward him, but bumped into someone.

"It's me," Corrine said.

"Sorry," I said, closing the distance between me and my father. He held out his hand for me to take.

"Micah," my father said, looking around, unsure of where to focus his attention. "Where is the entrance to the chieftain's quarters?"

"Make it halfway up," Micah said, "and you will see a number of open tunnels. Start walking down one, and it will lead you toward the center of the mountain. By the time you reach the first chamber... well, you should have met with a wolf already. As soon as you see one, start explaining your reason for being here. Their first instinct will be to attack you, but do all you can to avoid shooting flames."

"Understood," my father said. He looked down at me and nodded.

A cold hand squeezed my arm. Then lips brushed against my cheek. "Be careful." Caleb's voice.

"I will," I said.

Then a pair of cold arms wrapped around me. My mother this time.

I rolled my eyes. "It's okay," I said. "I'm going with Dad. I would probably manage even by myself."

My father tugged on me and we hurried toward the mountain. We looked around, wondering how to even start climbing up it.

"Look to your left," Micah called behind us.

We did, and that was when we spotted the beginning of a wide jagged staircase, etched into the side of the mountain. The steps were wide and very thick—clearly designed for wolves. My father's legs were long enough to climb them, but I found myself climbing them on all fours, as a toddler would. My father offered to carry me on his back, but I declined. I spent too much time on other people's backs.

I was feeling breathless by the time we were a quarter of the way up, despite my father and me having superhuman speed.

We paused, looking downward. My stomach lurched at how high up we were. The wind was harsher; it seemed to be getting stronger and stronger the higher we climbed. As a particularly strong gust passed by us, I was afraid that I might be blown away. I gripped the rocks so tight my knuckles grew white.

It was clear when we'd made it halfway up. The stairs gave way to a wide ridge and, as Micah had said, there were tunnels—lots of dark tunnels. I counted seven of them on our side of the mountain.

"Which do you think we should enter?" I asked.

My father pointed to the one nearest to us and led me through it. It was winding and narrow, though not too narrow for a wolf to comfortably travel down. The light outside of the tunnel soon disappeared as we traveled down several twists and turns.

The silence was eerie, the sound of my uneven breathing only adding to my nervousness. I clutched my father's hand tighter. The tunnel gave way to a large circular chamber with a high ceiling. It was dark, though unlike the tunnel we had just passed through, there were dim lanterns lining the walls. There was a strange musty smell that could only be described as *wolf*.

"Hello?" my father called out. When nobody responded, he called out again louder this time. Still no sign of anybody approaching.

"Micah said that we should have met one of the wolves by now," I said.

"We just need to keep looking," my father replied.

He pointed to the tunnel opposite us. I followed him as he crossed the chamber and entered through it. We passed along more twists and turns until we reached yet another, larger chamber. I could feel the damp of the walls, and it was colder here. I wondered how much further we would have to travel before we reached the center of the mountain.

"Hello?" we called out together.

Silence.

"Perhaps they are all out hunting," I murmured.

My father seemed to be distracted by something in the corner of the chamber. I followed his gaze. He was staring at a dark form crumpled on the ground. We moved toward it cautiously. It was a werewolf—in human form. That meant that the sun had risen on the horizon outside. He was a dark-skinned man, thickly built. The expression on his face looked like he was in pain.

"Excuse me," my father said, his mouth right above the man's ear.

The werewolf didn't budge. My father gripped one of his shoulders and shook him. Still no response.

"Odd," he said.

We continued along another tunnel. The chamber we arrived in this time was filled with more werewolves—men and women alike, all strewn on the floor and unresponsive to anything my father and I did to wake them. We even tried applying heat to their skin. After checking their pulses, we were certain that they were not dead, just in some kind of profound sleep.

I glanced up toward the ceiling, noticing that there was a level above us, lined with a low stone railing.

"Hey," I said suddenly.

"What?" my father asked, frowning.

"I swear I just saw something stir up there in the shadows," I said.

My father headed straight for the wall beneath the spot I was staring at. The wall's surface was rocky and jagged, allowing him to climb up toward the railing easily. He pulled himself over it with a thud and looked around.

"You see anything?" I asked.

I had barely finished my question when my father lurched forward and disappeared out of sight.

"Dad?" I said, holding my breath. "What's happening?"

There was a struggle, grunting and gravel crunching, and then my father spoke. "It's all right. I'm not going to hurt you."

"No! Let me go!" The voice was young—it sounded like that of a boy.

"It's all right," my father repeated. "I don't mean you any harm."

I was about to begin climbing the wall myself to see what was going on when my father reappeared. He was holding the arm of a small boy who looked no older than six. The boy struggled against my father's grip, but my father held on tight. The boy stopped suddenly when he saw me standing in the center of the chamber. His eyes widened. "You don't smell like witches. What are you?"

"We are Novaks," my father replied.

The boy wrinkled his nose. "Novaks?"

"We are here to help you," I called up. "We promise. What's your name?"

"Kyan."

"Can you tell us what happened here, Kyan?" my father asked.

"A w-warlock came." Kyan's voice trembled as he spoke. "He took my mother and my brother, and he cast a spell on our whole pack."

"A warlock?" my father asked, shocked.

"Yes. He's locked himself in the chieftain's quarters."

"Can you take us there?" my father asked.

Kyan bit his lower lip. "I am afraid to go near."

"Then tell us how to get there," my father said. "We might be able to help your parents if you help us."

"All right," the boy said after a pause.

My father helped him onto his back before climbing back down to the floor to meet me. Kyan pointed to a tunnel to our right. "Go down that passageway," he said. "It will lead you to another chamber surrounded by doors. The largest one is the entrance to the chieftain's private quarters... I-I don't know what the warlock wants with him."

"Thank you." My father looked at me grimly, then we left the boy and followed his directions.

Indeed, we did arrive in a chamber filled with rounded oak doors and we stopped outside the tallest one.

"Warlock," I breathed. "Who could that be?"

My father pressed an ear against the door and raised a finger to his lips. I pressed my head against the wood too and joined him in listening.

My heart skipped a beat as I picked up on a familiar voice, deep and masculine.

Rhys.

Chapter 13: Sofia

I was both relieved and surprised when my daughter and husband came climbing down the mountain so soon after they had left. I'd expected them to be much longer.

"What happened?" I asked, running forward as they approached, still invisible.

"We've got a problem," Derek said.

"What?" Kiev asked.

We all gathered around them.

"Rhys Volkin," my daughter replied. "He's within the mountain. He has taken the chieftain hostage."

Mona gasped.

"Are you sure?" Micah asked.

"Yes," Derek replied. "He has cast a spell on the entire

pack, except, it seems, for the chieftain. The chambers are filled with sleeping werewolves."

"What would Rhys be doing here?" Ashley asked.

I didn't know if Ashley's question was meant to be rhetorical or not, but we all concluded the same thing at once.

"He must be after Magnus too," Mona said, her voice unsteady. "He must want him for the ritual."

Her words were both panicking and comforting. If Rhys really had come here for Magnus in order to complete the ritual, then it meant that they hadn't carried it out yet. It had been so long since we'd left The Shade now, the thought of the black witches having already completed the ritual had been nagging at the back of my mind. If Rhys too was on the hunt for Magnus, then it meant that we might have time. But it also meant that we couldn't afford to let him find Magnus first.

"We have to knock the bastard out of the race," Kiev said.

"You forget that he is far more powerful now," Mona replied. "I have no idea how we would be able to pose a threat to him. We don't even have dragons."

"He has no idea we are here," Micah said. "Rose, Derek—is that right? He didn't see you?"

"No," Derek said. "We just listened in at the door. As far as I know, he is not aware of our presence here."

"Well," Micah said, "if he doesn't know that we are here, at least we have some advantage."

"Hardly," Mona said.

"Let's just get up to the mountain," Rose urged. "We have no idea how long he's going to spend with the chieftain. We can't let him get away. If he finds Magnus…"

We all knew the consequences.

Ibrahim, Mona and Corrine wasted no more time and transported us halfway up the mountain. The sheer height at which we were standing took my breath away. Rose and Derek pointed toward a tunnel and we began racing into it after them. We traveled through several tunnels and chambers, passing sleeping werewolves along the way, until we finally arrived in a room surrounded by wooden doors.

"That one," Derek whispered, pointing to the largest door a few feet away.

Derek and Rose vanished from sight—I was grateful that one of our witches had taken the initiative to do it.

"Let me to the front," Mona said. "I need to listen… It sounds like they are still talking," she whispered after a pause.

I didn't need to press my ear against the door to hear what was going on. Yes, they were talking, but it didn't sound like the conversation was going to last much longer.

"Because you know where he is," Rhys was saying, anger and impatience surging through his voice.

"I told you already," another male voice replied. "We have never come across a vampire named Magnus."

"You know what I will do to you if I discover you have lied to me," Rhys hissed.

We barely had time to formulate a plan before the door in front of us blasted open. I feared for a moment that Rhys had done it, but since he was nowhere in sight it must have been one of our witches. The sound of running filled my ears as we all dashed inside the chieftain's chambers. I barely took in the interiors of the wolf's quarters while we hurtled forward. We passed through a long passageway lined with doors and headed straight for the room at the end where the two men's voices were emanating from.

Rhys whirled round as a burning ball of blue fire shot straight toward him. A curse from Mona, I assumed. Rhys' face fell in shock, and then he vanished before the curse could hit him.

Oh, no.

A visible Rhys was terrifying enough, let alone an invisible one.

Where is Rose? Fear filled me as I realized I didn't even know where she was. The warlock could have been standing right next to her for all I knew.

The minutes that followed were harrowing. It seemed that none of us knew what to do. Spells hurtled around the room, and I kept expecting someone to be hit by a curse from Rhys and cry out in pain. The chieftain—a tall man with broad shoulders and flaming red hair—had spread himself out on the floor to avoid being hit by a spell.

After what felt like ten minutes had passed, I wondered why nothing was happening.

Mona spoke up. "I think he's gone."

"But why?" Aiden asked.

Mona appeared and then everyone else's invisibility spell lifted too, except Micah's. Since he had requested to be kept hidden at all times, I guessed our witches were being respectful of this.

Mona's face had paled and she sounded even more anxious than when she had first found out that Rhys had taken the chieftain hostage.

"Perhaps he has gotten what he needed," she said. Her eyes shot to the werewolf, still crouching on the ground. She hurried over to him and gripped his shoulders. "What did you tell that warlock?"

The wolf stood up, anger in his eyes. "Who are you people?"

"Not your enemies," she replied. "Just answer my question, or we will all be sorry."

"He wanted to know about Magnus," the chieftain growled, brushing Mona away from him. "I've never heard of such a vampire. And believe me, if I had, I would have revealed his location to that warlock. I despise vampires almost as much as I do black witches." He scowled, casting dirty glances at me and the other vampires present.

"So you have absolutely no idea who and where Magnus is?" Mona asked.

"No," he said.

Mona turned around slowly to face us, anxiety creasing her forehead. "Perhaps Rhys concluded that the trail is cold for Magnus here in this realm… Maybe we have hit another dead end."

"Why would he vanish so suddenly?" I said. "He has enough reason to want to stay and finish us all off."

Mona bit her lower lip. "Maybe he has gotten another idea… and his time is now too precious to waste on us."

Chapter 14: Mona

"Will you help to wake up the rest of my pack?" the chieftain asked, still eyeing us with suspicion.

I stared at the werewolf, my brain ticking over. "Yes," I replied. "But first you must agree to do something for us. Given the fact that we have just saved you, it should not be too much to ask."

"What?" he asked.

"Call a meeting immediately with the other chieftains so that we can ask them whether they know about Magnus."

The chieftain shook his head. "I truly doubt that any of us have come across a vampire named Magnus."

"I did not ask for your speculation," I said impatiently. "I asked you to arrange a meeting."

"I'm not on good terms with many of the other chieftains," he replied. "But all right. I will try."

"How long will it take?" I asked.

"At least three days."

I cursed beneath my breath. We didn't have that sort of time. I turned to face the others again.

"Can't you gather them any faster?" Derek asked.

The chieftain shook his head. "Impossible."

Three days—it was out of the question. It had occurred to me that perhaps Rhys had left to seek out another chieftain.

"Why don't you just magick the chieftain around this realm to make the traveling faster?" Rose asked me.

"Some packs aren't even here in The Woodlands right now," the wolf said. "At least two chieftains who cooperate with me are out on expeditions… As I said, I think you're wasting your time. No wolf here would tolerate a vampire's presence. You would be better off searching elsewhere."

Reluctantly, I saw sense in the wolf's words.

But where do we search next?

Where did Rhys go?

Although we couldn't afford to hang around now, Corrine, Ibrahim and I agreed to help the chieftain awaken his pack. Even though he was doing us no favor in return, I figured that there was no harm in befriending these wolves. It was good for them to see that not all witches and vampires were bad.

Once we had finished, we returned to the rocky shore where we had first arrived.

"And now?" Ashley said, the tone of her voice bordering on desperate.

I didn't answer, although I knew the question was directed at me. All eyes were on me now, waiting for my answer. I moved away from all of them and walked further up the rocks. I sat down on the edge, glad that nobody followed me. I didn't even want Kiev next to me right now. I just needed to be alone.

I took a deep breath, inhaling the crisp sea air and closing my tired eyes.

Magnus.

Where are you?

The fact that Rhys had left us so quickly when he should have at least caused some injury to us after the beating we had given his people in The Shade was deeply disturbing. I knew Rhys. If he was after Magnus, he would not stop until he found him. I didn't know whether the vampire was crucial to their ritual, but clearly he was important, otherwise Rhys would not be wasting Lilith's precious time searching for him.

We just seemed to be looking in all the wrong places. At least in The Blood Keep, The Tavern and The Cove we had managed to get some clue as to where to search next, but here… it seemed like we had met a dead end. Nobody had even heard of Magnus.

"What are we going to do?" Ashley repeated her question, and this time I answered. There was no point in denying it to myself any longer:

"I don't know."

CHAPTER 15: RHYS

Mona and her companions' appearance was certainly unexpected. And the thought that they were on to Magnus too was disturbing. But as much as it had been tempting to stay and finish them off, I had more pressing matters to attend to.

I did believe the chieftain when he told me that he did not know where Magnus was. Now I had to be sure that other chieftains hadn't seen Magnus either. Even if Magnus had befriended the werewolves, there was no way that they would risk their lives for a vampire. It just wasn't done by werewolves—at least not the wolves of The Woodlands. I traveled quickly from pack to pack, following much the same procedure as in the first chieftain's mountain. I eliminated all who were in my way by putting them to sleep. After meeting with the sixth chieftain, I stopped. None of them so far had seen a vampire named Magnus.

I have to rethink what I'm doing.

A feeling in my gut told me that even if I took the time—time I did not have—to meet with every single chieftain in this realm, I still would not find Magnus.

But where could that vampire have gotten to?

How could he have made it out of the realm without attracting the attention of even one werewolf?

Besides, he would have been weak on waking. He wouldn't have had any blood in years.

I had to think carefully about what my next step should be.

One option was just return to Lilith now, perform the ritual without Magnus, and hope for the best. But I hated the idea of yet another defeat. And we were much more likely to succeed if we had Magnus present. There was no doubt about it.

I have to find that damn vampire.

Having just left another pack, I entered the woods and paced up and down among the trees, breathing deeply and trying to clear my mind.

It was only after a few minutes that I realized that I had come full circle back to the mountain where I had put Magnus into slumber. I wasn't sure why, but something made me vanish myself back up to it. I entered through the open wall. I looked around the dark quiet chamber. I moved toward the open container where the vampire's body had lain.

I asked myself for what felt like the hundredth time: how had he escaped?

At the time, I had thought that I had secured him so expertly. Could I have been so delusional in my capabilities that even a mere vampire could escape my spells? I just could not believe it possible. As I looked around the room, I remembered how much effort I had put in to making sure there were no loopholes. Not even a skilled witch of the Sanctuary could have broken through the spells I'd put on this place. I was sure of it.

Now that I was taking more time to think—and I had recovered from the shock of seeing the container empty—I realized that I had acted too rashly before. Searching among the werewolves had been a waste of time. I felt like a fool. Of course they had not seen him.

Because Magnus had never escaped this chamber.

I should have realized what had really happened here right from the beginning…

Chapter 16: Mona

"You can't just say that," Ashley said. "We are relying on you."

I stood up, looking over them all with a heavy heart. "I can't lie to you. I have no idea where we go from here. We have hit a dead end."

Magnus could be anywhere within this whole supernatural realm—heck, he could even be back in the human realm. It was worse than trying to find a needle in a haystack.

And now we didn't even have any more leads. Not even a single straw to cling to that might lead us to his whereabouts.

"So what? We just... give up?" Rose asked.

"We can't give up," Derek said. "We have to end Lilith, or all that has happened until now will only be the beginning of our troubles."

"I don't know what you want me to say," I snapped. The pressure was getting to me.

Because I had spent so much time with the black witches and I knew most about them, it felt like the responsibility fell on my shoulders for leading everyone in the right direction. I wished that someone else could take on this burden for a change.

"Where is the nearest realm to this one?" Kiev asked. "Perhaps Magnus made it there, and perhaps they might have some clue as to where he is."

I was sick and tired of traveling from realm to realm, only to meet with more failure.

"But Kiev, for all we know that merman could have just been lying to us—hoping that the wolves of The Woodlands would finish us off. It's possible that Magnus was never anywhere near here."

I was about to slump down again on the rocks and bury my head in my hands to try to ease the headache that was now coming on full blast when a female voice spoke behind us.

"Excuse me."

We all whirled around and found ourselves staring at a short woman with long wavy hair. She had a red scar across her cheek.

"Yes?" I said, stepping forward.

"I heard what you are here for," she said. "You're here because you are trying to end the black witches, isn't that right?"

"Yes," several of us said at once.

"Well, I just spied that same warlock—Rhys—hanging around one of the mountains. I was the werewolf he first caught—he took my child hostage and forced me to lead him to my pack. He is still hanging around this place. I'm not sure what he's doing, but… I thought perhaps it might be useful to you since my chieftain cannot help you at all."

"He is still in this realm?" I asked, my mouth falling open. "How long ago was it that you saw him?"

"About ten minutes ago," she said. "I rushed straight here to see if you had left yet. I can take you to where I spotted him."

"Yes," I said, without even consulting the others. "Take us there."

It wasn't like we had any better ideas. We had hit rock bottom, and anything seemed better than standing here—even the prospect of meeting Rhys again.

We hurried with the female wolf to the spot where she had seen him. As soon as we arrived, we crouched down among the trees, making as little noise as possible as we peeked through the leaves at the nearby mountain.

"He was hanging around on one of those ridges," she whispered, pointing upward. "It's possible he is gone now."

"There is only one way to find out," I said. "I will go up there. The rest of you, stay down here." I didn't hang around long enough to give Kiev a chance to object.

I vanished myself as close as I could to where the wolf had indicated, keeping myself invisible in case the warlock was still up here. I was surprised to see a gaping hole in the wall. Before walking inside, I looked all around outside the cave—upward, sideways, downward—just in case Rhys was standing elsewhere. The last thing I needed was to get cornered by him.

When I was certain that he was nowhere in sight, I stepped inside the cave and looked around. It was empty, except for a long object at one end of the room. I approached it cautiously, and, nearing it, realized that it was some kind of casket. It was empty and lined with a thin sheet. I bent down closer, examining the ridges and then the interiors. I caught sight of something black and very thin within one of the folds of the sheet. I thought at first that it might be the leg of a spider, partially obscured by the fabric. But as I straightened the sheet, I realized that it was a black hair.

"I sense vampire in here." A voice spoke behind me, causing me to almost jump out of my skin.

I breathed out in relief to see that it was just Micah.

"I figured that you might be able to make use of my sense of smell," he said.

He approached and peered down over my shoulder. Clutching the hair in my hand, I walked toward the exit so that I could see better.

Micah, who had followed me, dipped his head down and sniffed the hair. We locked eyes, and he nodded. "That is the hair of a vampire."

My heartbeat quickened as a theory came crashing down on me at once.

"Rhys hid Magnus in here," I breathed.

I walked back over to the container and studied its edges more closely. I could tell in ways that an untrained eye couldn't that this casket had once been sealed by a spell. I hurried back to the open wall, examining the edges of the entrance, and could see the same thing here—Rhys had secured this place.

"Why was Rhys looking for Magnus if he was supposed to be in here all along?"

"Magnus must have gotten out somehow." I backed into a corner and slid down along the wall, thinking furiously.

If Rhys had imprisoned Magnus, it made total sense. He was valuable to Rhys—almost as valuable as Lilith herself. Because if something ever happened to Magnus, she would be at risk.

But then what happened to the vampire?

I knew how strong Rhys was—even if he had brought Magnus here many years ago when he wasn't as developed in his powers, he had still been a powerful warlock. Powerful enough for a vampire to be unable to escape.

Micah tried to talk to me again, but I silenced him. Now more than ever, I needed to be lost in my own thoughts. It did not take me long to realize what must have happened.

Because there was only one way Magnus could have broken Rhys' spell.

Someone more powerful than Rhys must have set Magnus free.

I shot to my feet.

I knew exactly where we had to go now.

The Sanctuary's graveyard.

Where this journey started.

Where it must end.

Chapter 17: Isolde

What the hell is that man thinking?

If my nephew had told me that he would be gone this long, I never would have agreed to it.

Lilith had already woken up, and I was expecting her to ask to begin the ritual at any moment. I had been avoiding going inside her chambers, and I had told Julisse to do the same. We just made sure to make ourselves available if she called for us. Truth be told, I'd thought that she would have called us in long before now to say that she was ready.

She had needed some time to recover and adjust to her new body, but I was surprised that she didn't feel prepared by now. As strange as it was, I didn't pay it too much thought. I was just grateful that she was taking her time.

We could only hope that Rhys would hurry up, and that nothing had happened to him.

I knew the value that Magnus's presence could bring to the ritual—of course I did—but the fact was that we could still do it without the vampire. The chance of success would just be somewhat less.

I found myself unable to sit still and instead paced up and down the castle corridors, thinking over all the details of the ritual we were about to perform and ironing out everything in my mind until I felt confident that I hadn't overlooked anything.

I had been so wrapped up in my own thoughts and worries, I had not noticed someone approaching behind me. I jolted as a voice spoke my name. My voice caught in my throat when I saw that it was Lilith. Standing in all her youthfulness, she wore a dark dress trimmed with lace that clung tight to her shapely body. I still had not gotten used to seeing her like this—I still saw the skeletal form I had been around for too many years to count.

I was surprised to see her out of her room. Until now, she had always requested that we go in to see her.

"What can I do for you?" I asked, even as I anticipated her answer. *She is ready for the ritual. What else would she have come out for?*

"I would like some more time alone before the ritual," she said, her voice smooth and pleasing to the ear.

I barely believed my ears.

"Oh, of course," I said, "you should take as much time as you need to prepare."

She nodded slowly. "I… I shall be gone from this castle for a while—though I don't anticipate being gone much more than a day."

This was even more strange. I couldn't imagine where she would want to go outside the castle. But I wasn't about to ask. I was just relieved that she wasn't ready to start the ritual yet. If she had said that she was, I would have no way to explain to her why Rhys wasn't here. I wasn't willing to tell her about Magnus— at least not yet. Nobody knew how she would react on learning that her order to stay away from Magnus had been disobeyed. We ought to wait until the very last minute before revealing him—once the ritual had already commenced and she was less likely to protest.

"Of course, your Grace," I said, bowing my head slightly. "We will be here waiting for your return."

It felt like a heavy weight lifting off my shoulders as she disappeared from sight… to whatever destination it was she had in mind.

CHAPTER 18: LILITH

I stood at the edge of the pool that had served as my resting place for centuries. I removed my shoes and placed them on the floor. Then I dipped into the liquid for the second-to-last time. Submerging myself, I pushed myself deeper and deeper, passing along my portal. When my head surfaced above the fluid, I wiped the thick substance from my eyes and looked around the familiar room. It was almost identical to the one I had just exited from, but this chamber… it was sacred to me. Only two people had ever set foot inside. It had been that way for centuries, and it would remain that way forevermore after tonight.

I lifted myself out of the pool. The chamber was bare and empty but for a raised platform in the center upon which stood a bed lined with pure white linen. Curtains hung around it—closed, as I always left them when leaving this place.

Climbing out from the grime, I cast a charm to clean myself and changed into new clothes. A white gown that matched the bed linen.

My heart raced, as it did every time I approached this bed. I fingered the curtains nervously, as if doing this for the first time, and then pushed them aside all at once.

Even now an ache stirred within me on seeing the vampire lying there, eyes closed, breathing gently. He was in the same state now as he had been when I first took him in.

I moved closer, brushing my hand against his cool cheek. A part of me still felt guilt over keeping him here with me. When Rhys had come to me all those years ago, asking for permission to hunt down Magnus, I had refused to give it. But I had suspected at the time that Rhys would disobey me. I had been correct.

Once I'd discovered where Rhys had hidden Magnus, I had intended to wake and release the vampire immediately. I hadn't planned to bring Magnus back to my sanctum. But on seeing him for the first time in so long, the thought of letting him go had been too much to bear, the idea of his presence so close to me too tempting. The pleasure I'd begun to derive from his company—albeit silent—had far outweighed the guilt I felt. So I'd kept him with me.

Of course, it wouldn't be forever. I'd known that when I'd first laid him to rest down here and that had also made the guilt less crushing.

This would just be like one long dream in his immortal existence. A blip in time. And when the right moment arrived, he would wake up and continue the life he'd had before. Perhaps with a new lover.

I glanced back down at the black pool in disgust. Long thin handprints—from my wasted body—stained the edges of the pool as well as the ledge just beneath Magnus' bed, from when I would prop myself up out of the liquid to watch him sleep.

There was no place for such darkness in here now. Not on our last night.

With a wave of my hand, I cleaned away any signs of grime from the floors and then transformed the black liquid in the pool into crystal-clear water. Discontented with the bare walls, I manifested hanging pots filled with luscious flowers and sweeping vines, and arranged them all around the room. I fixed softer lighting to the ceiling so that a haze of light emanated down, giving the illusion of early-morning sun trickling through nonexistent windows. Then I lined the floors with silk carpets and placed four pots of burning frankincense around the bed.

Once I was satisfied that the room was in a fit state for

Magnus to wake up in, I approached the bed again and walked around it, stopping directly behind his head. I flattened my palms against his forehead, brushing back his dark hair and placing a kiss on his skin.

I moved my lips down the bridge of his nose, then reached his lips. My whole body shivered as I relished the feel of them. It was the first time that I had kissed him since the night I'd told him I could no longer be his. Although many things about my past blurred in my memory now, I would never forget that final meeting. The expression on his face, his anguish, and my helplessness to do anything about it still remained etched in my mind.

I kissed him harder.

I hadn't had any choice then.

But tonight… Tonight would be different.

It would be my last night with Magnus, but in many ways also my first. The first night of my existence when I would not feel guilt for loving him. Because after the ritual, I would be no more anyway.

I placed my hands on his broad shoulders and ran them beneath his pale cotton shirt. The feel of his chest beneath my fingers made my body ache for him.

It's time to wake up, my love.

Finally, it's time to wake.

I dipped down again to kiss his lips and this time, I brought him to consciousness. His eyelids quivered, then shot wide open. My heart pounded as I stared down at him, deep into his blue eyes that I had not beheld for centuries. They had the same effect on me now as they'd had the first the day I'd met him.

"Lilith?" He stared at me in shock.

My name coming from his lips was nectar to my ears.

"Yes," I breathed. "It's me."

"Where am I?" he whispered.

"In a dream."

Gripping his head, he sat up in bed. I walked around to the foot of the mattress, content with just watching him.

"A dream," he muttered, still gazing at me as though he expected me to vanish at any moment. "This doesn't feel like a dream."

I bit my lip, wondering whether to tell him the truth. If he believed that it was a dream all along, once I was finished saying goodbye to him I would put him to sleep and take him away to someplace safe, and he would wake up believing that it had indeed been a dream. But if I told him the truth, it would make parting all the more painful.

I decided not to respond to his comment and let him believe what he would.

"We don't have long," I said softly. "There's something that I would like to tell you… something I never got a chance to say before."

He frowned, then, swinging his legs off the bed, stood

up and walked over to me. His eyes blazed down into mine.

"What?"

I detected hurt in his gaze as he asked the question. I was sure that he too was remembering the last time we had seen each other.

"I love you," I said before my voice could choke up. "I always have."

His frown deepened, his voice hoarse as he replied: "Then why did you leave me?"

His words were like a dagger through my heart.

"I-I told you. I had no choice."

"You could have run away with me," he said. "We could have escaped, traveled far away and started our lives over. Nobody would've had to find out about us."

My shoulders sagged. Magnus didn't understand. He never did. Perhaps if I had belonged to a lesser family I could have escaped. But I couldn't have gotten away with it with my family.

"You didn't love me enough," he concluded from my silence.

You don't know how much I love you. You never will know, was what I wanted to say.

"Perhaps... Perhaps I did not love you enough," I managed. "But now it's different. Tonight... I'm free."

I swallowed back the lump in my throat as he reached up to my face, his thumb brushing against my cheek as he scrutinized every part of my face.

"I just wonder," I said in a voice barely louder than a whisper. "Do you still love me?"

His eyes narrowed. My stomach clenched as he broke eye contact for the first time since he had woken up. His gaze settled on a spot on the floor. But it was only for a moment. When he raised his eyes to me again, fire had ignited behind them.

He answered my question by backing me up against the bedpost and claiming my lips. He kneaded his against mine as his hands began to roam freely along my body. My heart felt so light, I barely knew how to handle such joy. I kissed him back with as much passion as my black soul could muster, hoping that it would be enough to satisfy him. When I began to unbutton his shirt, the action triggered a spiral that soon found me lying flat on my back against the mattress. Magnus crouched down over me, kissing me with more hunger than I knew how to respond to.

It felt as though every touch we exchanged, every kiss, every embrace, only added to the bonfire that now blazed between us. All the pain, the guilt, the frustration that I had harbored within me for so long melted away and all that was left was an all-consuming heat. Magnus' strong body brushed against mine. Our bare forms were entwined as close to each other as we could possibly be. And for once, it felt like he held my heart too—not just a part of it... but all of it. My heart beat only with love for him.

"Magnus," I panted through his kisses, "you're the reason I'm still alive."

He raised his face to look at me, his lips flushed with the little blood he had in his veins.

"What do you mean?"

"If I didn't love you, I would not be here with you now. My love for you was strong enough to keep me alive centuries past my natural lifespan."

"What are you—?"

I raised a finger to his lips, wrapping my legs tighter around his waist.

"I don't want to waste our precious time telling you the whole story. Please… just promise me that whatever happens to us after tonight… you won't ever doubt that I loved you."

There was a pause, his passion still pulsing deep within me.

A heavy burden lifted from my chest as he moved his mouth next to my ear and whispered:

"I promise."

CHAPTER 19: ROSE

Kiev looked like he was about to go climbing up the mountain after Mona and Micah by the time they finally reappeared next to us.

"What happened?" my father and Kiev asked at once.

"We need to head to The Sanctuary's graveyard," Mona replied.

"Why?" Corrine asked.

"I believe that is where we will find Magnus."

"Huh?"

"Rhys imprisoned Magnus in a cave up in this mountain. But somehow the vampire got out, otherwise Rhys wouldn't have been going to such lengths to look for him. The person who let Magnus out had to be more powerful than Rhys. And I believe that person was Lilith. Isolde is powerful, but I don't see what reason she would have for letting Magnus out."

"Lilith," Kiev said.

"I know how much she loved him," Mona continued. "I experienced it through her memories. If she indeed did take him, there is a chance that she has kept him with her."

"In The Sanctuary's graveyard?"

Mona nodded. "I know that he is not being kept in her chamber on the island Isolde and Rhys arranged for her… Look, you just need to trust me on this. We have no time to lose. For all we know, Rhys could be heading there right now."

We all huddled around, not daring to ask any more questions even though my mind was burning with dozens more. And before I knew it, we had all vanished.

Opening my eyes again, I found us standing on a beautiful beach. We faced the wide-open ocean. Behind us were tall trees lining the shore, and to our left were rock formations.

Mona headed straight for the line of trees and we followed her. As she was about to enter the woods, she jolted back, as though she had just bumped into something.

"They have extended the boundary," she said, rubbing her head. "Let me try to break through this. I was able to last time I was here…"

We all stood back to give her some space as she began trying to break through. When she still hadn't managed to after five minutes, we all knew that something was wrong. She turned around to look at us, her face ashen. "Ibrahim, Corrine. You can try to help me. But something has changed since we last visited here. Stronger reinforcements have been put up around this place."

Ibrahim and Corrine walked forward to help her, but even with their efforts combined, they were no more successful.

I jumped as a sudden banging filled the air. It almost sounded like a gunshot and it seemed to have come from about a mile away.

Mona, Corrine and Ibrahim cast an invisibility spell over all of us again as we looked toward the sound. We began clambering over the rocks for a better view.

"Oh," Mona said softly a few feet in front of me. I hurried forward to see what she had spotted. And then I gasped myself.

Standing in the middle of the beach beyond the rocks was the warlock we had just left behind in the werewolf realm. His wavy hair tucked behind his ears, he was hurling powerful-looking curses toward the boundary. It seemed that he had not noticed us yet. And we needed it to stay that way for as long as possible.

We needed to get inside the boundary quickly, and now

it seemed that neither Mona, nor Corrine, nor Ibrahim would be able to pull it off.

Only I could.

We backed away from watching Rhys and leaned against the rocks in a row.

I stood up. "Corrine, can you remove the invisibility spell, please."

"Why?" my mother and Corrine asked at once.

"Please just trust me that I'm asking for good reason."

I was pleased when it was removed a moment later.

"You guys wait here and keep watch on Rhys' movements," I said. "I'm the only one who can get us inside. Give me about half an hour. I'll do my best to return within that time."

"But where you going?" my mother asked.

"I need to try to attract someone's attention on the inside of the boundary. I think it's better if I just go alone. I'll be heading along this beach—just try to keep Rhys away."

With that, I began racing away before anyone could try to hold me back.

The truth was, I had no idea where to start. At least this side of the island was bordered by forests, but I couldn't start yelling out in case Rhys heard me. No, I had to travel further away from here where I could raise my voice without fearing being overheard. Rhys was not a vampire or a werewolf, so I hoped that his hearing would not be sharp enough to pick up on me from miles away.

The sand whipped against my heels as I raced forward across the beach. I kept my eyes on the lines of trees, hoping that they would start thinning the further I ran. But they were showing no signs of disappearing. Heck, if anything, it appeared that they were growing thicker. My heart sank as the sand gave way to piles of rocks. I could still climb over them, but it would not be as fast as running across flat sand. Heaving myself up, I began clambering along, careful not to slip and injure myself in the process. *At least there are no giant crabs.*

Instead of trees to my left, now there was just a solid wall of rock—I was at the foot of a cliff. I craned my neck upward and paused for a moment. I moved along the rocks and tried to approach the wall of the cliff, but found that I met an invisible barrier about three feet away. I'd been hoping to climb up it. No chance. I had no choice but to continue forward in the same direction.

About a mile up, the rocks gave way to more sand—and yet more trees. The trees were no thinner than before, but as I stopped to listen, I could hear distant talking. There were people not too far away. I felt that I was at a safe enough distance to begin calling out. I crossed the sand and walked as close to the woods as I could without hitting the barrier and began yelling at the top of my voice:

"Hermia Adrius! I need to speak to Hermia Adrius!"

I yelled for what seemed like five minutes straight until my voice felt hoarse. I looked up and down the shore, hoping that someone would come. But nobody did.

Either nobody heard me, or they were ignoring me. I doubted the former was true—if I could hear them, they should have been able to hear me screaming unless the barrier was soundproof. But I didn't see any sense in that—it would only block them off from warnings of an attack.

It seemed that there was only one way to find out.

Time to try a different tactic, I think.

"The Sanctuary is under attack!" I screamed, in as panicked a tone as I could. "The black witches are here! You are all in terrible danger!"

That should get someone's attention...

And sure enough it did. Only one minute after I stopped yelling, an elderly-looking warlock emerged through the trees behind the boundary. His eyes were wide with worry as he looked me over.

"Who are you?" he asked.

"I am Rose Novak, an acquaintance of Hermia Adrius, and she will be furious with you if you do not escort me inside the boundary and bring me to her this instant."

"Novak, you say? How do I know you are who you say you are?"

I was about to suggest that he just go and fetch Hermia

and bring her to visit me, but I didn't like the idea of losing sight of him in case he disappeared and decided not to return. I wanted to be taken to that witch, and I wanted it now.

"Do I look like a black witch to you?" I asked, cocking my head to one side.

He shook his head.

"Then what are you afraid of? I'm just a girl. A human. I am no threat to you."

When he still hesitated, I lost my patience. "Look, warlock, I saved the life of the sister of your Ageless. The least you can do is let me inside."

He still appeared doubtful, but to my relief, he stepped forward, crossing the boundary and grabbing my hand before pulling me inside.

He was looking at me as though I was about to wield some magic on him, or perhaps transform into a black witch.

"It's okay," I said. "I am who I say I am."

"I will take you as far as the Adriuses' palace. But I will not bring you inside. You will wait outside the gates."

"Okay," I said.

He caught my arm and we vanished. We reappeared outside an ornate set of gates, beyond which was a magnificent palace made of pure white marble.

"Wait here," he said, looking at me sternly before he

disappeared from sight.

I did as requested, looking up and down the quiet road. There were two other warlocks standing guard outside the gate who were looking at me suspiciously. I slipped my hands into my pockets, avoiding their gaze.

I was surprised when Hermia appeared before me only minutes later. I was expecting to wait much longer.

"Hermia," I said. "I need your help."

She raised a brow. "What's wrong?"

"Firstly, you may or may not be aware that Rhys Volkin is outside on one of your beaches trying to break into The Sanctuary. I'm not sure what spell you put up around this place, but it's doing a good job."

From the look on Hermia's face, it seemed that she had not realized that Rhys was attacking.

"Secondly, I'm here with my family, Mona, Corrine and some others. We need you to let us inside. Right now. I don't have time to explain everything—it's an extremely long story, but if you don't let them enter, you are going to regret it sorely."

"Mona?" Her mouth hung open.

I realized that I was talking fast, and it was a lot to take in, but I felt impatient all the same.

"You remember what I did for you? I hope you have not forgotten already."

Her eyes darkened. "Of course I have not forgotten. I

will be forever in debt to you for what you did for me and my fellow witches that night."

"Then just trust me on this and let my people inside. They are waiting on the beach, near one of the rock formations. And we need to go to the graveyard."

"The graveyard?" she said, looking even more confused.

"Are you just going to stand here all day repeating my words? Please, hurry."

Composing herself, she nodded. "Very well," she said. "I trust that your people will do no harm to us. I will let them inside."

I described where I'd left them as best as I could, and then I locked arms with Hermia so she could transport both of us there. We appeared on the beach, and sure enough it was the right one.

"They are all invisible," I began, "but they should be waiting just over—"

"Rose!" My mother's voice drifted across the beach—not from the direction of the rocks, to my surprise. It had come from the opposite direction. She no longer had an invisibility spell over her and I could see her racing toward us.

My heart sank, instantly assuming the worst: Rhys.

I've just about had it up to here with that warlock.

I would've taken great pleasure in tying him up and burning him at the stake.

"Where is everyone else?" I asked as she reached us.

"Rhys started causing problems," she said. "I stayed behind on this beach to make sure someone was here when you came back. But everyone else is trying to head Rhys off just beyond those rocks over there."

"We don't have time to waste on that warlock now," I said, grinding my teeth in frustration. "We need to get Mona and everyone else to the graveyard."

"Without letting Rhys inside," Hermia said, her face paling.

"Will you place an invisibility spell on the three of us?" my mother asked, addressing the witch.

"Yes," Hermia said, and it was done a moment later.

I reached for my mother's hand, then for the witch's. We hurried across the sand and over the rocks.

A sandstorm had engulfed the area, particles of dust blowing in all directions. I shielded my eyes with my fingers to prevent more particles from flying into them.

"Everyone is in that?" I gasped.

"Yes," my mother replied. "I don't know how Rhys detected us, but he did. Mona conjured up this storm to make aiming curses more difficult. We need to somehow get everyone's attention without attracting Rhys. We can't afford to make him aware that Hermia is here with us or he will head straight for her."

Hermia shuffled uncomfortably next to me.

"Hermia," I said. "You stay here. My mother and I will go in and start trying to gather people, and then you must escort them immediately through the boundary."

"I will wait here," Hermia replied. "Just be careful. If I sense Rhys heading my way, I'll have to re-enter the boundary without you. I can't risk being caught and him gaining entrance to The Sanctuary."

My mother and I both continued over the rocks and touched down on the sand on the other side.

The full force of the wind against my face now was dangerous. I had to close my eyes for fear of being blinded. There was a tearing sound next to me and I felt my mom's hands around my head, tying a piece of fabric so that it protected my eyes, nose and mouth from the brunt of the wind. When I touched the cloth, it seemed like she had just ripped it off from the bottom of her shirt. It wasn't easy to see through it, especially in this storm, but I could just about make out the ground a few feet in front of me. Everyone was invisible anyway—there wasn't a lot to see. I would have to find my way by watching the ground for footprints. Of course my mother had her acute sense of smell. She could keep her eyes closed and still find people without problem.

"Hopefully vampires will detect your blood and start making their way toward us," she breathed.

We waited in the same spot for a minute, but when

nobody approached us, we had no choice but to move forward.

I kept my eyes focused on the ground in front of me as far as I could see, holding the fabric tight over my mouth so that nothing entered it.

I was glad when my mother let go of me so we could go in separate directions. It would make things faster.

The first footprint in the sand was only about two feet away from me. And more footprints were being created as I looked down. I heard heavy breathing—it sounded like that of a female. I reached forward and felt cold skin.

"Rose?" Ashley had scented my blood.

"Come with me," I hissed.

I dragged her away and raced with her toward Hermia by the rocks, leaving her there and trusting that Hermia would do as my mother and I had requested.

Then I rushed back toward the stormy beach. The next footprints I spotted were large—clearly that of a man. I stopped in my tracks, holding my breath and listening for any clue as to who this was.

A hand reached out and touched me. It was warm. "Rose?" It was Micah.

I hurried back over with him to Hermia.

"Has my mother returned with anyone since?" I asked.

"Yes," she replied. "Quite a few. Your father, grandfather, and several others. She and your father are on the beach now searching for those remaining."

"You remember Caleb, right?" I said. "You saw him with me that day you came for us on the boat. Has he returned?"

"I don't think so," she replied.

I backed away and moved back into the storm. I guessed that Mona must still be out here too causing this commotion. Perhaps she was keeping Rhys occupied.

It took me much longer to spot more footprints this time. *Caleb should have sensed my blood by now. Why hasn't he made his way over to me?*

Finally, I noticed indentations in the ground about five feet away. Again, they were large, as Micah's had been. These could have been Caleb's. Or they could have been…

My stomach plummeted as the footsteps approached me. I barely had time to stumble back before a hand reached out and grasped my arm. The moment it did, the warlock appeared before me and I realized that I too had been made visible again.

Instinct took over and fire coursed from my palms, forcing him to shoot back away from me. His eyes sparked with fury and he glared down at me.

"Rose Novak." As he raised his palms, I was about to hurl myself in the opposite direction when a heavy weight crashed into my midriff, making me fly several feet away from the direct aim of the warlock.

Arms wrapped around my body and lifted me off the

ground. I was whizzed across the beach with lightning speed. The fabric my mother had tied around me flew off and I was forced to cover my eyes with my hands. But I didn't need sight to know that it was Caleb. I knew my fiancé too well by now. His scent, the way he breathed... I could recognize his presence even in the darkest of nights.

I cast a glance over his shoulder toward where we had left Rhys. To my horror, he had begun following us. He was so focused on the two of us that he didn't notice a green ball of fire fly toward him from his left—from Mona's palms, I could only assume—until the very last minute, when he flattened himself on the ground just in time.

"Mona?" I called out. "Come!"

Caleb reached the rocks with me and I guided him to the spot where we had left Hermia. To my relief, she was still standing there waiting for us. I didn't understand why I'd been made visible on coming into contact with Rhys, but I was grateful for it because it helped Hermia spot us faster.

She grabbed hold of us and vanished us away from the spot. We reappeared again behind the boundary, in a clearing near the woods, when Hermia left us again. I looked around to see the rest of our companions. Mona, thankfully, appeared about a minute after us, Hermia and my parents by her side.

The invisibility spell over each of us had been lifted by now, allowing me to see the state of everyone. Mona looked in the worst state, her hair a disheveled mess, with cuts and burns all over her skin. Most everyone else just looked red raw from the sand, as I was sure I was.

Mona swallowed hard and turned her gaze on Hermia. "I don't know what that warlock is going to do now. But mark my words, sooner or later, he will find a way to break into The Sanctuary. We need to head straight for the graveyard. And you must go to all lengths to make sure that nobody disturbs us."

CHAPTER 20: RHYS

I had no idea how the white witches had managed to put such a powerful spell around The Sanctuary that even I was having difficulty breaking through it. I was on the verge of returning to get reinforcements when rocks crunched in the distance. At first I thought that someone from The Sanctuary must have been spying on me. Little did I know that it would turn out to be Mona and her companions.

Mona was smart to have figured out where I was headed. I couldn't deny that about her. Now there was not even a shadow of a doubt that she was after Magnus just as I was. I could not allow her to reach him first. I did not know what she intended to do with him, but I assumed she meant to kill him.

I launched an attack, but as had happened too many times before in the past, Mona slithered out of my grasp. She was like a mosquito I never could manage to swat. But she had been lucky too often—partly due to my own weakness for her.

Now that she was posing a direct threat to Lilith, that luck would end soon.

After losing them, I forced thoughts of the witch out of my mind and focused on reaching our castle as fast as I could. Arriving outside, I stormed through the main entrance and searched for my aunt. I found her sitting in her room at her desk, a book open on her lap, though she did not appear to be reading it.

She looked up as I entered and shot to her feet.

"Rhys? What took you so long?"

There was relief in her voice, but also anger.

"There's been a complication. Several complications."

"What are you saying? We cannot afford complications."

"Magnus was not where I left him," I said.

"Then let's just forget about Magnus and perform the ritual without him." She gripped my shoulder hard. "We do not need that vampire. You even admitted it yourself."

Ignoring her comment, I asked, "Has Lilith woken yet?"

"Yes," my aunt replied.

"Where is she?"

I was surprised when Isolde hesitated. "I… I don't know

exactly. Lilith said that she needed more time to recover before the ritual. She left this castle, but she did not tell me where she went. Honestly, I was just relieved that she was not ready to start the ritual."

This odd behavior from Lilith was further confirmation of my suspicion of Magnus' whereabouts.

"When will she return?" I asked.

"She left hours ago," Isolde replied. "She did not specify when she would return, but she said that she was unlikely to be more than a day... but Rhys, let's forget about—"

"Listen to me," I said, my voice a growl. "I need you to gather up ten other witches. We need to leave for The Sanctuary."

"The Sanctuary?"

"The graveyard in The Sanctuary. We both know that Lilith has a second chamber beneath her tomb there that she never allows anyone to enter. I stored Magnus in the werewolf realm, and somehow she managed to find out what I'd done and retrieve him. I believe that she's been keeping the vampire there all along."

Isolde's lips parted as realization dawned on her. "That certainly would explain why Lilith spent so little time in the chamber we had constructed for her... But why would she do this?"

"Why wouldn't she do this? We both know her love for Magnus. I don't know how she found out I'd imprisoned him, but I'm not surprised that she took him with her. His proximity must have added to her strength. We have all been surprised at how long she has managed to last. This must be one of the reasons—she has had Magnus so close to her all these years." I pulled up the sleeve of my shirt and began healing a wound as I spoke quickly. "Lilith only ever surfaced on our side when we needed to speak with her. And she deliberately closed off the portal connecting to the cave whenever she was in her sanctum beneath her grave. We need to reach The Sanctuary and find the vampire."

Isolde frowned. "What you're saying makes no sense. If Lilith wanted Magnus to take part in the ritual, she would have said by now. She clearly doesn't want that. We can't force her."

"Of course we can't force her. All we can do is try to reason with her. But the ritual isn't why we need to find Magnus any more. Mona is after him."

Isolde scowled as soon as I spoke the witch's name. She never had liked Mona even before the witch had betrayed us.

"We must stop her."

Chapter 21: Mona

I got chills every time I entered The Sanctuary's graveyard, and this time was no exception. I led everyone straight to the back where the ancient tombs were located until we reached Lilith's grave.

I turned to Hermia. "Station witches and warlocks around the graveyard to make sure we aren't disturbed."

Once she had agreed and left, Rose murmured, "So this is Lilith's grave," staring at the ancient tombstone with a mixture of horror and fascination.

I bent down and placed my hands over the stone lid. I'd probably been just feet above Lilith last time I had been here… if I'd just dug past her coffin I might have reached her.

I didn't waste any more time and forced open the lid. A dark bed of soil lay beneath—the same soil I'd dug up last time I'd been here. Ibrahim and Corrine helped to dig up the earth faster and soon the lid of a mahogany coffin came into view.

I lowered myself into the hole and slid down the side of the casket. I placed my hands underneath its lid, gauging how loose it was. Before lifting it open, I looked up to see Corrine, Ibrahim and Kiev beginning to make their way down after me.

It was cramped enough as it was, so I told them to stay where they were. At least for now, only one person could take this journey. Any more, and we would just attract attention—something we could not afford. None of us would have a chance against her if she decided to wield her magic. I had to see what was down there first.

I popped open the lid. It was still empty. I stripped the coffin of all the fabric and linen that was lining it until I reached the wooden base.

As much as I despised it, I lifted myself into the container. Crouching on all fours, I pressed my ear against the wood, listening for any kind of sound coming from below.

There was nothing. No indication of any life beneath. Just silence.

But I knew better than to give up. Perhaps it was

covered over now, but I knew that there was a portal somewhere around here. Lilith had once pulled me through it the same night I'd murdered the Ageless in her sleep.

"What are you doing?" Kiev asked.

I ignored his question. I didn't know what I was doing.

Using my magic, I drilled a hole through the base of the coffin. It was large enough to put my whole head inside. To my dismay, there was only soil beneath. I began digging deeper into the earth and when I found that I was digging up nothing but more earth, a nagging doubt entered my mind that perhaps I had gotten the wrong end of the stick yet again. But the knowledge that Rhys had headed to The Sanctuary too reminded me that I couldn't have.

This place must hold the answer.

I spent the next few minutes in silence, ignoring questions called down toward me by Kiev, Derek, Sofia and others. Finally, I reached my first glimmer of hope—a dark, shiny substance. Thick liquid.

I looked back up and nodded at Kiev and the rest of my companions. "I'm onto something now," I said. "But you must stay up there. No matter what happens, no matter what you think might be happening, don't come after me. It will only make the situation worse."

The look on Kiev's face pained me. I'd given him cause for grief on so many occasions recently, I had lost count. I just hoped that this would be one of the last.

Still using my magic, I expanded the hole in the floor of the coffin enough for my whole body to fit through. I dug away more of the soil underneath until I could slide right through and dip my feet into the glistening substance beneath. But before I lowered myself down, I stripped down to my underwear. I didn't want to have any extra weight. I remembered how dense that liquid had been.

Casting one last glance upward, I dropped myself down.

I winced as my feet made contact with the substance. It began pulling me downward immediately, like quicksand. It reached my waist, my chest, my neck… I barely had time to utter a spell that would allow me to survive for an extended period of time beneath it before it engulfed me completely.

At first I was pulled down slowly, but then I began to gather speed. After what felt like a minute of sinking, I began to wonder how deep this liquid really was. After three minutes, a fear took hold of me that perhaps the only way to successfully travel along the portal was with Lilith's permission.

What if this liquid leads nowhere? What if it's never-ending? Just an abyss of endless slime?

I shook myself. *Get a grip.* It's only been a few minutes.

Still, the thought haunted me.

My tension eased only slightly when I realized that the liquid seemed to be getting less thick, and I was beginning to pass through it much faster. It also felt less grainy and abrasive against my skin. Then my feet hit something solid, and my whole body bent as I passed along some kind of rounded tunnel. I emerged against a flat surface. I stretched out my hands to feel around—it felt like stone. I gathered my legs beneath me and kicked up hard—though I was still too afraid to open my eyes in case they stung. Although this liquid felt much lighter, I didn't know that it was any less toxic.

Only daring to open my eyes once my head poked above the surface, I wiped my face with my hands and looked around.

I was shocked to see that not only was I in water, it was the clearest, most pristine-looking water I had ever seen my life. It looked purer than even the lakes of The Sanctuary, and there was not a single trace of the dark muck I had just passed though.

I kept my head low as I took in the magnificent chamber I'd emerged in. There was a fragrant smell of incense. Soft light emanated down from the ceiling, and exotic-looking plants and flowers decorated the walls. Lining the floors were luxurious carpets and in the center of the room was an elevated platform upon which stood a large four-poster bed. I almost swallowed my tongue as I realized that I was not alone. I dipped down back into the water as quietly as I could, the vision I had just witnessed etched in my mind's eye. Although the curtains had been drawn around the bed, they were thin enough for me to make out a man and a woman, wearing nothing but sheets, wrapped in each other's arms. For a moment I feared that they might have heard me, but they had looked so absorbed in each other, I realized that the fear was likely unfounded.

Lilith.

She had her youthful form back.

I wondered what the meaning of that was. It didn't take me long to form a theory.

My heart hammered in my chest as I sank down as low in the liquid as I possibly could.

I have to talk to Magnus.

But first, I need to get him on his own.

Chapter 22: Mona

How am I going to do this?

Daring to approach the edge of the pool again, I stole another glance at the bed. The couple still seemed too lost in each other to detect my presence.

Then I looked more closely around the room, racking my brains for ideas. When my gaze fell on a burning pot of frankincense in a far corner of the room, a plan formed all at once. I took a few moments to think it through, wondering if it could really work. It was so risky that it made my stomach flip just thinking about it, but I couldn't see any other option right now. And there wasn't time to keep thinking.

Desperate times call for desperate measures.

I rested my eyes once again on the burning pot and stared at it intensely. I repeated a chant in my mind, careful not to let any of the words slip from my mouth. When a small cloud of smoke billowed up from the mouth of the pot, I knew that I'd been successful. The smoke was followed by flames that began to swallow up the pot and climb higher and higher up the walls in the space of a few seconds.

Lilith and the vampire sat up straight and stared at the fire. Draping a sheet over her shoulders, Lilith slid herself off the bed and made her way toward the blaze.

Casting an invisibility spell over myself, I leaped out of the pool and padded silently to the bed. Magnus had his back to me as he sat watching Lilith approach the fire.

It was surreal to be finally standing within a few feet of this vampire we had just traveled through realms to find, only to be unable to say even a word to him.

Tearing my eyes away from Magnus, I hurried to the head of the bed where the pillows were. I spotted what I had been seeking. A short black hair. I hadn't kept the hair I'd found back in the cave, but even if I had, this one would be more potent. I picked it up and examined it closely, making sure that it couldn't possibly be from one of Lilith's strands. Certain that it wasn't, I clasped it between my fingers before hurrying back toward the pool.

Lilith had now dealt with the fire and was walking back

to her lover. I slipped into the water noiselessly and sank beneath the surface, reaching the bottom. I ran my hands along the ground, but this time I kept my eyes open, looking for the entrance to the chute I had traveled through. I spotted a dark hole in one corner. That had to be it. I swam toward it, pulling myself through it.

Now that I no longer had gravity on my side, I needed to use the force of my magic to propel myself upward.

I passed through water for a couple of minutes, then grimaced as it showed its first signs of becoming murky. It wasn't long before I was wallowing in thick slime again. I couldn't let up for a moment in pushing myself upward, or I would start sliding downward.

Even though I knew that the grime was thick, I was shocked at how much effort it was. I was beginning to feel tired. I checked the hair in my fingers by squeezing them together several times, worried that I might have lost it on the way. But I hadn't. I was holding it so hard I was beginning to lose sensation in my fingers.

When my head finally poked above the surface of the liquid, I breathed in deeply.

"Mona." It was Kiev's voice, filled with relief. He was standing inside the casket. He reached a hand through the hole and pulled me to my feet. We climbed together out of the grave and onto the grass.

"What happened?" several people asked at once,

including my husband.

I didn't have time to explain now what I had to do. I just had to do it.

"Just wait for me here, okay?" I said.

I caught Kiev's hand and vanished with him, leaving everyone else behind. Kiev looked utterly confused when we reappeared in the grand spell room within the Adriuses' castle. I was glad to see that it was empty.

When I walked over to the sink, the first thing I did was wash Magnus' hair, rinsing off the grime. I placed it down on the table top before proceeding to gather together all the ingredients I needed.

"Are you going to tell me what happened to you?"

"I found both of them down there. Magnus and Lilith. The problem is I can't get to Magnus while Lilith is there. She knows I betrayed her. One look at me and she could burn me to ashes."

Kiev stood next to me by the cauldron I had just placed on the stove and was beginning to pile ingredients into.

"So what are you doing?" he asked.

"I'm creating a potion that can make me look like Magnus."

Kiev's jaw fell open. I remembered now that Kiev had likely never encountered such a potion. When Sofia had used it to bring reconciliation between Derek and Kiev, she had requested us never to tell Kiev about it and to this day we had honored that request.

"I don't understand," he said. "Why?"

"Because we need to separate Magnus from Lilith."

"But how will this help?"

"I will need either Corrine or Ibrahim to come down to help me. I can't say exactly how we'll pull it off now. We need to see what they are doing once we go down again. But the plan is to replace myself with Magnus so she won't notice that he is gone."

"Wouldn't it make more sense if I became Magnus and the two of us went down together?"

My voice caught in my throat. "Kiev, this is so dangerous."

"All the more reason for me to become Magnus instead of you."

I realized that Kiev's suggestion made sense on another level. I knew the most about Lilith's history with Magnus, more than I could possibly explain in the time we had available. It made sense for someone else to become Magnus, while I attempted to persuade him to help us. Still, I couldn't help but feel hesitant to agree to Kiev's proposal. The thought of leaving him down there with the witch chilled me.

"I can't stand you going down there without me," he said. "I hate having no idea what's going on."

"Okay," I sighed. "You take this potion instead of me

and we will both go down together."

I still felt conflicted even as I poured the potion into a cup and handed it to him.

"Drink it all," I said.

Once he'd finished drinking, he said, "Next?"

I walked over to the hair on the tabletop and picked it up.

"Open your mouth," I said.

He did as I had requested, but before I placed the hair on his tongue, I kissed him.

"I don't like this," I breathed.

"We will be doing this together," he replied, returning my kiss with passion. It seemed that was all the comfort he was going to offer me. Not that there was much more he could say.

I drew away and placed the hair on his tongue.

"Just keep it there," I said. "Don't swallow it."

I placed my hands either side of his head and began uttering a chant. Once I was finished, I let go and watched him closely for the first signs of transformation. I didn't have to wait long. His eyes were the first thing to change—they turned from green to blue. Then the rest of his facial features followed—his jaw, nose, forehead—before his limbs adjusted to Magnus's physique. He was about the same height as Magnus and was also similar in build, so other than his face and hair, not much had changed visibly.

There was no mirror in the spell room so Kiev couldn't see himself.

"You are Magnus now," I said, once I was sure his transformation was complete.

He looked down at his clothes. "I'm still wearing my own clothes."

I shook my head darkly. "You don't need to worry about clothes."

He frowned, then looked uncomfortable. Clearly he hadn't thought this through.

"We will undress you once we get nearer," I said. I did, however, reach for his hand and remove his ring, tucking it into my pocket. I hated the thought of him alone in bed with that witch, even in the form of Magnus. But we had done this now. There was no time for second thoughts.

"Undress me? Mona... once we arrive, what do I do exactly?" I could detect the nervousness in his deep voice. Something that was unusual for Kiev. He didn't usually show much emotion.

"We need to first observe the situation as it stands and take things from there... But you're going to have to avoid talking as much as possible."

"I'm not touching that hag," he said, his lip curling with disgust.

Despite the situation, I couldn't hold back a laugh at Kiev's reaction. He was still thinking of Lilith as a walking corpse.

"Then you may have to get creative while Magnus and I are gone."

Chapter 23: Mona

When I arrived back in the graveyard with Kiev, everyone stared at him in shock.

"Meet Magnus," I said grimly.

"Mona gave me a potion so I look like him," Kiev explained. "It's odd having two arms again…"

"So Magnus is definitely down there?" Sofia asked.

"Yes," I replied. "He is there now with Lilith. We're going back down now, and this time, I hope to return with the real Magnus."

Kiev and I made our way back into the grave and stood together in the coffin. I lowered myself down through the hole I'd dug leading to the slime, and pulled him down after me, keeping a tight hold on his hand. Before we submerged, I put a spell on him and myself again so that we could survive beneath the surface without breathing.

And then we began our descent to Lilith's sanctum—my second visit, Kiev's first.

I didn't let go of Kiev's hand even for a moment as we traveled through the liquid. I could sense his tension and I was sure that he was having similar doubts as I'd had on my first journey down as we sank deeper and deeper. For me at least, it seemed to go faster this second time. Soon we were sliding through the chute and had appeared at the bottom of the clear pool of water. Kiev's first instinct was to kick upward, but I pulled him back down. I placed my thumbs over his eyelids, tugging them gently upward to indicate that he could open them.

I held a finger to my lips, then pointed upward. "Let's go," I mouthed silently.

We bobbed up to the surface and the first thing I did was look toward the bed. I was terrified that they might notice us appearing, but no. They were still in bed. This time, they both lay still. Apparently they had tired each other out and were resting in each other's arms.

I raised myself out of the water, indicating to Kiev that he stay put. I replaced the invisibility spell over myself and neared the bed. Lilith was facing the opposite wall, while Magnus had an arm around her waist. They were still close, but at least it seemed to be a neutral position for Kiev to be in. That would make this an easier job for him.

But I was still worried by their closeness. He was holding her quite tightly. There would be no avoiding her noticing him withdraw from her on the bed. We just had to make sure that Kiev placed his arm around her quickly so she didn't notice it too much.

Holding my breath, I walked back over to the pool, now indicating that Kiev follow me. He climbed out of the pool silently. I dried off his—Magnus'—body first, then helped him remove his clothes without making a sound, keeping my eyes firmly on his face as I did. Then we moved to the bed, standing on the side closest to Magnus. My pulse racing, I just wanted to get this over with. I first wrapped a hand around Magnus' mouth, then silenced him with a spell. Before he could writhe around, I paralyzed his body, made him invisible and levitated him off the bed.

I was relieved when Kiev took the cue, quickly and gently placing himself on the bed where Magnus had lain while I moved with the real Magnus back toward the pool of water. Lilith turned slightly at the commotion. When she eyed Kiev, I stopped in my tracks, unable to even breathe. Then she turned back round, reaching for Kiev's hand and holding it closer against her.

Thank God.

Slowly and carefully, I sank with Magnus back into the pool and made him follow me though the chute, through the portal leading back up to the grave. As we traveled, the whole time I was thinking of my husband and praying that he would not be caught. Of course, Lilith had the power to reveal his true form if she suspected something, but hopefully she would have no reason to. I just had to be as quick as I could with Magnus.

As soon as my head emerged through the base of the coffin, I lifted myself up, making Magnus levitate above me. Now that we were out in the open, I removed the invisibility spell. Everyone stared at Magnus. His limbs were constrained, though his face was filled with alarm and anger.

"Kiev is still down there," I said. "Make sure you stay here."

With that, I vanished Magnus and myself from the spot. I had already thought about the best spot to talk with him—somewhere that was far from the grave, yet at the same time would give us ample privacy.

We re-emerged on the rooftop of the Adriuses' palace. I planted Magnus down a few feet away from me, then, keeping his legs paralyzed, I gave him back control of the rest of his body. Sitting against the wall, he glared daggers at me. I walked to the edge of the roof and looked over it. Noticing an open balcony beneath, a curtain blowing in the wind, I tore the fabric from its railing with my magic and handed it to Magnus so that he could use it to preserve at least some modesty.

"Who are you?" he snarled, tying the cloth around his waist. His blue eyes flashed at me as he bared his fangs.

I breathed out slowly, trying to collect my thoughts.

Now the real work begins.

CHAPTER 24: MONA

"I am someone whom you need to listen very carefully to."
I approached him cautiously, squatting down so that my
face was level with his.

"What do you want?"

I paused, wondering how to even start getting through
to this vampire. I didn't know just how much he loved her,
but in bed earlier, he'd seemed to be completely absorbed
in her. Whether that was lust or love remained to be seen.

I could try to force or torture him into submission, but
the change in attitude toward Lilith had to come from his
heart, if he was to break hers. She would detect any
insincerity on his part.

"First, I need to explain to you what and who Lilith

really is."

"I know more about Lilith than you could ever know," he shot back.

"I don't doubt that you *knew* Lilith, but do you really know her now? You seem to be unaware, vampire, that you've been asleep for centuries."

He looked shocked. "Centuries?"

"Yes. Lilith kept you imprisoned beneath her grave. Rhys Volkin—one of Lilith's accomplices—was the one who first caught you and put you to sleep. You really don't remember being caught?"

He frowned, then shook his head. "Why should I trust a word that comes out of your mouth? You still haven't even told me who you are."

"My name is Mona Novalic. I used to be a black witch, a part of Rhys' clan. I was even inducted as a Channeler by Lilith. But I left their cause because I've had a glimpse of the destruction that they will cause not only to the human realm, but all realms if they take over The Sanctuary and rise to prominence."

"Mona Novalic," he repeated slowly, then muttered, "This isn't a dream." He rubbed his head and blinked hard.

"This is certainly no dream," I replied.

"Lilith and I parted ways long, long ago, on the understanding that we would never see each other again. She was the one who requested that we stop seeing each other. What reason would her accomplice have to seek me out and put me to sleep?"

"Good question," I said, relieved that we were starting to have open dialogue. "Magnus, first you need to understand that Lilith used you. The love that you once shared, she took advantage of and used in a spell to keep herself alive and extend her lifespan far past its natural course. Had it not been for you, she would have been dead long ago. Rhys kidnapped you because you are most valuable to them. He didn't want anything to happen to you, otherwise Lilith risked losing her own life. The only reason you are in contact again now with her is because she needed you. Had she not found use for you, I doubt she ever would've bothered speaking to you again."

He cleared his throat, shifting uncomfortably on the ground. "Even if what you're saying is true," he said, sitting up straighter against the wall, "why are you telling me this? How can I trust you?"

"As I said, I'm working to stop the black witches. They are about to perform a ritual which, if successful, would have repercussions for all creatures weaker than them. That includes vampires. I have already had a glimpse of the horrors they can inflict on others, and I do not want them rising to prominence. The reason I took you from the chamber is that I need you to help us. Lilith is key to the ritual because she is the last Ancient living among us.

Without her, I doubt they will ever grow stronger than they are now."

There was a pause. I stared at the vampire, trying to read his expression. It seemed quite blank, though his eyes had darkened. "I would trust more what you're saying if you would release me from this curse you have me under," he said, looking down at his paralyzed legs.

"I'm sorry," I said, before obliging.

He kicked his legs and got to his feet. He walked closer, towering over me and looking me over intensely before beginning to pace up and down in front of me.

"I've known all along the type of magic Lilith practices," he said. "That has never been a secret from me. Black magic runs in her family. It is no surprise to me that all this is happening now, many centuries later—if you are indeed telling the truth and centuries have passed. I lived in those days when the Ancients ruled. When vampires and all other creatures avoided crossing paths with them at all costs. I only came across Lilith by chance... and, as fate would have it, we fell in love. In my view, if they carry out the ritual with Lilith, the situation will be no different now than it was then. I'm already used to living in hiding, in solitude. Nothing you've said has convinced me I should help you."

My stomach sank, and I hesitated before asking my next question. "Do... Do you really still love her?"

His eyes fixed on his feet, then he turned his back on me

and stared out at the beautiful view of The Sanctuary the hilltop palace afforded.

"Yes," he said finally. "I love her now, just as I loved her before."

"So the fact that she manipulated that love for her own personal gain means nothing to you?"

He didn't answer my question. He just remained silent.

"You do realize that the form she's in now is artificial," I pressed. "It's not her true form. It's just a mirage, covering the darkness and evil that she has become—"

He scoffed. "Don't talk to me of darkness and evil. I'm a child of the Elders, for Christ's sake. Cruor was practically my birthplace. I've seen more darkness and evil than you will ever witness if you live ten thousand years." He turned around to face me. "I don't see where this conversation is going."

"Magnus, you have not experienced what it is like to live without the Ancients reigning supreme. It seems you've never experienced a life without hiding and living in anxiety. You don't know freedom. If you did, you would be fighting alongside us and doing whatever it took to prevent the black witches from rising to power again. Will you allow me to give you a taste of what your life could be if you agreed to help us?"

"It could be like heaven. I don't care. It's not reason enough for me to work against Lilith."

I was beginning to feel desperate. As much as I hated myself for it, the words Xavier had spoken before we left The Shade flitted through my mind:

"Do we have to kill Magnus in order to end Lilith?"

I had dismissed Xavier's suggestion at the time. I'd said that all we needed to do was break Lilith's heart. Because I hadn't wanted to even consider the idea of murdering another person. I had enough blood on my hands already. Now the question haunted me: what if I couldn't get Magnus to cooperate? Should I just let him go? The consequences of that action could mean countless more deaths.

What if we have to sacrifice his life in exchange for saving innumerable others?

No. I can't murder again. I just can't do it.

The lives I'd claimed in the past still haunted me at night sometimes. I couldn't bear to add to that list.

I have to get through to this vampire somehow.

"Magnus," I said, fighting to keep my voice steady. "Did you not hear what I said about Lilith using you?"

"I heard you," he said. "But whatever motivation she had for keeping me alive doesn't change the past we shared, nor the fact that she still loves me. You admitted yourself that she would not be alive if it weren't for the strength of her love for me that keeps her heart beating."

Damn you, Magnus.

I racked my brain for what else I could say to convince

him.

Maybe I just need to show him what she actually looks like now.

Paralyzing him again, I pushed him back against the wall and placed my hands on either side of his head. Summoning the memory of Lilith in her true corpse-like form, I surged the vision into his brain through my fingertips. His eyes shut tight as the image blasted through his mind. Once I was sure that he'd had enough time to take it in, I let go again, watching closely for his reaction.

To my dismay, he hardly blinked.

"That is Lilith's true form." I grabbed his shoulders and shook him. "Don't you see the abomination she has become? You allowed her to become like this."

"Perhaps."

"Perhaps what?"

"Perhaps that is her true form now. Perhaps the night I just shared with her was simply an illusion. But… I still remember the girl she was. The woman I loved. I'm not willing to go against her."

I was about to lose myself in desperation when a thought occurred to me. "Do you remember the night Lilith left you?"

"Yes," he said, his jaw twitching.

"What do you remember of your life after that night? What did you do when she left, and you thought that she was gone forever?"

He furrowed his brows again. "I don't see what business that is of yours."

"Did you not love anyone else since Lilith? You must have, Magnus. You can't have just—"

"No. I have never loved a woman as I have loved Lilith."

Oh, dear.

I was running out of things to say, and it seemed that he was running out of willingness to engage in this conversation.

Now I realized just how stupid I had been to even think that I might be able to undo a lifetime of love and attraction in just one conversation.

In one way, I couldn't blame Magnus. He was in love with Lilith—a love that was so strong it blinded him to all else. Either that, or his heart was as black as Lilith's and he really did not care what happened if the black witches succeeded.

Whatever the case, I'd run out of ideas as to how to get through to him.

I took a step back, staring at him. He glared back, his eyes filled with defiance.

Again, the words Xavier had spoken passed through my mind.

The darker part of me was once again tempted to just finish him off. I was more powerful than this vampire. It would not be difficult to finish him off with a curse and dump his body in the sea. But I just could not bring myself to do it.

He'd never done anything to harm us directly, and he was posing no threat to me now. Even if killing him could have saved countless others, I wasn't the person to do it. Not any more. I'd sworn to myself that I'd given up that life when I'd arrived in The Shade. I simply wasn't willing to drag myself back to my dark past.

Instead, another plan began to take shape in my mind. A plan I'd wished with every fiber of my being that we wouldn't have to resort to.

But before I lost myself in worrying about our next step, first I had to take Magnus somewhere safe and out of the way. I didn't have time to start venturing out of The Sanctuary to find some hiding place. I had to find somewhere within this realm that was safe.

"Release me now," Magnus said.

I ignored his command and looked around at the view from the rooftop. My eyes fixed on to the distance—past the city and the suburbs.

Then I approached Magnus on the floor again. I silenced him once again with a spell so that he couldn't shout out, then made him invisible before placing a hand on his shoulder. I vanished us both and we reappeared again at the bank of a river. There was a waterfall crashing down a few hundred feet away, and the river churned and flowed so rapidly that it was impossible to see the riverbed from the bank. Casting a third spell over Magnus to ensure that he could remain comfortably beneath the water even if I left him there for two days, I levitated him off the ground and sank him into the water, deeper and deeper until he touched the bottom. Then I dove into the water after him and swam down toward him so that I could see what I was doing. Ripping off a piece of the fabric tied to his waist, I fastened it around his ankle and knotted it around the root of a tree that grew deep in the riverbed. This would ensure he didn't bob to the surface in his paralyzed state. There were no dangerous creatures in these waters that would bother him. So he would just remain here beneath the water until I was ready to return.

Once I was satisfied, I was forced to turn my mind again to the plan that chilled me to the bone.

God help us.

If we pull this off, it will be nothing short of a miracle.

Chapter 25: Kiev

I was relieved when Lilith turned her back on me and faced the opposite wall. At least she hadn't noticed me replacing Magnus. Even just feeling her back leaning against my chest, her hand resting on top of mine, repulsed me.

Granted, she was not nearly as hideous as I had expected. But I still despised everything about this woman. She could be the most beautiful woman on earth and I would still find her presence repulsive.

She made no motion to do anything other than hold my hand for the next few minutes. But then she turned back around again. I looked down at her reluctantly. I was not sure how my emotions were coming across through Magnus' face. But I did my best to conceal them.

Her dark eyes locked on mine and a small smile formed on her lips. To my horror, she reached her hands around my neck and began leaning toward me.

My hand shot up and I pressed a finger against her lips just in time. I couldn't stand kissing her even with Magnus's lips.

I was surprised by the strength of her grip around me. Her frame seemed thin and frail.

She frowned at me.

"What is it?" she asked softly.

I felt mad for saying it, but it was the only thing that I could think of to get out of that kiss.

"I would rather spend our time talking now," I said, even as I recalled Mona's warning to avoid talking at all costs.

Her smile broadened. I was relieved to see that my response had pleased her. She sat up, sliding her hand in mine and tugging on me to sit up next to her on the mattress.

"You are right," she said. "We don't have much longer." She paused, tucking a strand of hair behind her ear. "I always did wonder, what happened to you after that night we parted? Where did you go?"

"I paid a visit to my sister," I said, with as little hesitation as I could manage. Ernesta was the only thing that I knew about Magnus's life in any kind of depth.

"I see," Lilith said.

"I didn't stay with her long. I've never gotten on well with my sister. I spent time in The Cove after that."

"Why The Cove?"

Good question… I couldn't imagine any vampire in his right mind wanting to spend any amount of time in that insane place. I wasn't sure where a vampire could physically live in that place in any case…

"I met a girl… a mermaid." I was fully aware that I had just made my story even more bizarre, but I had already dug myself into a hole. I wasn't about to stop digging. "I managed to find a dark cave to stay in, away from the sun."

"Oh," she said. A flicker of pain played across her face.

I was surprised by how easily she accepted the explanation. I wasn't sure how a vampire could even have a relationship with one of those creatures, even if he could bring himself to look past her black teeth and slimy appearance. Lilith seemed to be too affected by the idea of Magnus being with another woman to think much into my story.

I supposed that was good. We needed to break her heart. I still didn't know how Mona planned to do it, but I figured that making Lilith feel jealous and planting the seed that Magnus had been with other women since her could only help.

"I didn't stay long in The Cove either," I continued. "I

soon realized we weren't very… compatible."

"And then what happened to you?"

"I met another witch. I was in a relationship with her up until Rhys came for me. After that… I remember nothing."

She breathed out deeply, raising my hand against her lips and planting a kiss against it. "I'm glad that you managed to find someone else, Magnus," she said. "I was living in guilt that I might have cut you too deep to heal."

"Yes, I was very much in love with her," I said.

She swallowed hard, but nodded. She even managed a smile. "Good. That makes me happy."

I gazed into her eyes, surprised at how she was responding. It seemed that she really did care for Magnus. She wanted him to be happy.

She averted her eyes away from mine. "We need to part soon, Magnus. And I will probably never see you again. I hope you'll move on again with your life, as you were able to before. I just… I wanted to see you again before I passed away."

"Passed away?" I asked, genuinely curious.

"Yes," she replied. "I told you already that I shouldn't have lived this long. My time is coming soon. I've been granted this last burst of youth, but after this, I'll no longer be able to fight death's clutches."

I found it interesting that she deliberately left out the fact that she was about to perform a blood ritual. Perhaps she didn't want Magnus to know about the evil she was about to engage in.

"I promise that I will look for the witch I fell in love with and continue our relationship, if she'll still have me."

She smiled again, and then I sensed that she was about to lean in for another kiss. I was saved by a splash from the pool at the other side of the chamber.

Relief was the first emotion to rush through me, but then I was consumed by alarm. My first thought was that it was Mona. But I should have known that it wouldn't be her. She never would have been so careless as to draw Lilith's attention.

No, emerging from the pool was none other than Rhys Volkin.

Chapter 26: Mona

Leaving the river, I transported myself back to the graveyard. Approaching Lilith's grave, I was shocked to see that nobody was surrounding it. I'd told everyone specifically to wait here.

What's going on?

It was then that my attention was drawn to shouting in the distance. My eyes shot toward the borders of the graveyard. It was teeming with crowds of witches and warlocks. Bright curses lit up the sky, hurtling in all directions.

The graveyard was under siege.

And that could only mean one thing: Rhys had returned with reinforcements and the black witches had managed to penetrate The Sanctuary's boundary.

Of course, the black witches were weaker outside of their own territory. They were completely outnumbered and wouldn't be able to do much damage, but it would only take one of them to slip through the defenses…

"Mona!" I turned around to see Aiden approaching me, worry written on his face. His words confirmed my fears. "Rhys has returned with more witches. They managed to break through the boundary. The white witches are doing a decent job of heading them off, but we have lost sight of Rhys himself."

"When was the last time you saw him?" I asked, my fists clenching.

"About five minutes ago. We've been looking for him ever since among the crowds, but none of us have spotted him since. We fear that he might be—"

I didn't wait to hear the rest of his sentence. I leapt into Lilith's open grave and dropped through the hole in the base of her casket. I submerged myself in the liquid and let it drag me downward. I was so panicked that I had not thought to put the breathing and invisibility spells over myself before leaping in, so I cast them now before I reached the base of the pool.

Please, Kiev. Please be all right.

Reaching the water, I pushed myself up slowly, careful to cause as few ripples as possible in case someone was watching the pool. I poked my head above the liquid and looked around the room, my pulse racing.

Magnus—Kiev—was standing a few feet away from the bed, holding a sheet up against him. In front of him stood Lilith, also holding a sheet wrapped around her for modesty. And in front of her was the warlock. Rhys.

I kept myself submerged as low in the water as possible while still being able to hear their conversation. I wanted to call out to Kiev to reassure him that I was here—I could only imagine how vulnerable he must have been feeling with these two monstrously powerful witches in the same room. He was just a vampire—his only protection was his disguise, which could be removed at any moment if either of them suspected something odd about him.

But so far, it seemed that they hadn't...

"No, Rhys," Lilith said, glaring at the warlock. She'd planted herself protectively in front of Kiev.

"I am merely making a suggestion," Rhys said. I could tell that he was trying his best to reel in his temper.

"And I have already given you my answer," Lilith said, looking no less aggravated than Rhys. "You had no permission to kidnap Magnus. I had forbidden you to go near him. We will perform the ritual without Magnus. We do not need him."

"I understand that we do not need him," Rhys countered. "And I apologize for disobeying you. But please understand that I had your best interest at heart. You are not as strong as you used to be, even though you are in your youthful form again. Nobody knows what the strain of the ritual will do to you—remember, we have never attempted anything like this before. I merely want to improve our chances of—"

"No," Lilith said, "I want you to leave. I never gave you permission to seek me out in my sanctum. Yet another thing you have disobeyed me in."

Rhys' back heaved. "As you wish," he said. "I hope that you do not live to regret this decision."

"I will not," she snapped.

"Before I leave," he said, "there is something you must be aware of. Mona is after Magnus. You must make sure that he is safe. Somehow she managed to find out about him…"

"Mona." Lilith spoke my name as though it was a dirty word. "Fear not. I will make sure that Magnus remains protected for as long as the ritual lasts. Nothing will happen to him, and nothing will happen to me." She looked the warlock right in the eye. "We *will* complete the ritual without him… So leave now. I will meet you back in the castle soon so we can begin."

I began to panic as Rhys started moving toward the pool. I backed away from the entrance of the chute as far as I could. I held my breath as he got inside and kicked toward the hole. I hoped that he wouldn't sense my presence in the water. Thankfully he didn't. He disappeared through the chute.

I raised myself back to the surface to see what was happening with Kiev and Lilith. She had approached him and had begun talking to him.

"The time has come for us to part, my love." Her voice was choked up.

Kiev looked down at her seriously through Magnus' blue eyes.

"I will cast a spell on you," she said, "a strong spell, and nobody will be able to lay a finger on you for five days. That will be enough time for you to get away from this place to safety. I've arranged for a boat on the northeast shore of The Sanctuary, which is where you are now. I'll take you there myself."

She moved closer to Kiev and wrapped her arms around his neck, pulling him down and closing her lips around his. I couldn't help but feel a twinge on seeing her passion, although technically she was kissing Magnus.

The kiss lasted for what felt like three minutes. Kiev had tensed up and was trying to ease away from her, but she kept pulling him back, kissing him harder and running her hands along his back.

When she was finally finished, she manifested a set of clothes for Kiev to change into—which I imagined that he was deeply grateful for. Then she manifested a set of clothes for herself—a long dark dress.

Once they were both wearing clothes, she gazed back at Kiev.

"One last thing," she said. Reaching for the collar of her dress, she pulled it downward, exposing her neck. "You haven't had fresh blood in your system for a long, long time. Drink from me now. It will give you strength."

Kiev hesitated, but it didn't seem like Lilith was going to let him off the hook, so he wisely did as she had requested.

He placed his hands either side of her waist and sank his fangs into her flesh. He tried to withdraw after a few seconds, but Lilith insisted that he drink more, so he did.

After what looked like ten deep gulps, she finally let him go. Kiev wiped his bloody mouth against the back of his sleeve, grimacing.

"Now," she said. "I will cast the spell on you."

She made him bend down before her on his knees. Grasping his head, she began muttering a chant even I could not recognize. It sounded long and complex. Whatever it was, I was grateful that she was casting it on Kiev. At least I didn't have to be worried about him getting hurt during whatever we were up against next.

As tears began spilling down her cheeks, it dawned on me just how much she loved Magnus. She was willing to sacrifice the very cause she had devoted her life to for him.

Having Magnus present at the ritual could have improved the chances of being successful, yet she had shunned Rhys' suggestion. I never could've expected such emotions from her.

She kissed Kiev once more, long and hard, and then the two of them vanished.

The northeast shore. I tried to picture their destination in my mind before vanishing myself too.

I appeared on a beach, but it was empty. Clearly I'd gotten the wrong one. I scanned all the beaches in the area until I finally spotted a boat bobbing on the waves in the distance.

Standing next to it was a tall dark figure. Kiev. But Lilith was nowhere in sight. She must've bade her final goodbye to him already and left to begin preparation for the ritual.

I hurried toward Kiev and whispered, "She's gone?" just to be sure.

"Yes," Kiev replied, looking in my direction.

I manifested myself again so that Kiev could see me. Relief spread across his face. We motioned to embrace each other, only to find that there was some kind of invisible barrier between us.

Frustration surfaced within me. All I wanted to do was hold him. Still, it was a good thing that he was so... contact-proof.

"Now what?" Kiev asked.

"We need to hurry back to the graveyard to gather the others," I said.

Since the black witches had already broken through The Sanctuary's boundary, and it seemed that the white witches had not yet put it back up, we had no problem re-entering the city. We raced together to the graveyard and as we did, we began discussing what our next step had to be.

Our next, and hopefully final, step.

Chapter 27: Mona

When we reappeared in the graveyard, it was evident immediately that the struggle with the black witches had ended. There was no shouting, and no sign of any curses being hurled about. White witches were milling around the tombstones.

"Mona," Derek called behind us.

"They've gone?" I asked.

He nodded. "They just… withdrew."

As the ocean withdraws before a tsunami…

"We need to gather everyone around," I said. Kiev and I had already worked out exactly what we needed to do now. The run had been useful. We had been able to clear our heads and discuss the situation without distraction.

A few minutes later, all of our companions were surrounding us. Kiev and I were bombarded with questions about what had happened, but we were able to go into detail on only the things that were essential to know.

"We need to reach the black witches' castle in the supernatural realm," I said. "That is most likely where they are carrying out the ritual."

"Will we even be able to enter?" Erik asked.

"Let's just see what happens when we get there," I said.

Corrine and Ibrahim didn't know where the island was. Only I knew. I recalled making this journey when I was younger, from The Sanctuary to their small island, when I had been banished.

"Wait… How will I travel there?" Kiev asked.

I frowned at him. "By magic, of course—"

My voice trailed off as I realized I couldn't touch him. I looked around the graveyard, my eyes settling on a nearby tree. I walked over to it, snapped off a branch, and then placed it on the ground at Kiev's feet.

"Pick it up," I told him.

He reached down and picked it up.

"Now try to touch me with it," I said.

He extended an arm and was able to touch me with the end of the branch.

"Okay," I said, relieved. "Keep the stick against me. This should work."

I made sure everyone else was touching before transporting everyone to the black witches' island. Thankfully, Kiev wasn't left behind. Arriving, we found ourselves standing in a cluster of giant black rocks, the ocean lapping close to our feet. Yes, there was a boundary keeping us out. I realized that this boundary I would not be able to penetrate. I decided not to think about how we were going to enter for now. First we needed to locate where they were holding the ritual.

I knew enough about the witches' habits to guess that the ritual would be held outside. There was no room inside the castle that would have been large enough to hold all the witches as well as all of the blood that they would need.

"I smell blood. Lots of blood," Caleb whispered.

The other vampires murmured in agreement, as did Micah.

"Which direction is it coming from?" I asked.

Aiden pointed to our right, further along the rocky shore. We made our way toward the smell until it was so strong that all the vampires and Micah stopped at once.

"We are right next to it," Matteo said.

We then moved as close to the barrier as we could before we hit up against it. But we were still too low down to see anything from this angle. Corrine, Ibrahim and I lifted ourselves into the dark night and hovered above the boulders to get a view of what was happening.

My eyes widened at the scene beneath us. A massive vat that looked more like a lake was filled with deep red liquid. Blood. Lining its edges were piles of humans. Mostly young females and clearly alive, they were hogtied with ropes. Crowds of black witches stood around them, holding ceremonial knives. I spotted Isolde, Julisse, Rhys and some other familiar faces, but couldn't see Lilith yet. Somewhat of a good sign. At least it meant that they had not yet started. Still, it was clear from the scene that it wouldn't be long now.

When I lowered myself again, I was shocked to see that Kiev had managed to cross the boundary.

Could that be the effect of Lilith's spell on him?

"Kiev," I whispered. He stepped back through it and approached me. "Okay. We'll wait out here for you. But stay with us until Lilith arrives—I'll give you the signal."

Levitating myself in the air again, I looked back down at the scene to see how it had progressed. Lilith still hadn't emerged. I wondered what was keeping her. I found myself glancing from the area, then back down to Kiev, afraid that he might suddenly turn back into himself. He had shown no signs of it yet, and since I'd taken one of Magnus' head hairs—as we had learned from experience when Sofia had been stuck in the form of Derek for more than a day—it was more potent and it should last a long time. I just hoped I hadn't brewed the spell any differently than before.

"Is that her?" Corrine whispered, hovering in the air a few feet away from me. I couldn't see what she was pointing to at first, but then I noticed. The witches surrounding the lake to our right were parting, making way for Lilith, who had changed, now wearing a pure white dress that trailed down to her feet. She was walking toward the pool. Her long dark hair hung down her shoulders, and it had been braided with thorny twigs—from a rose bush, I guessed. Clasped in her hands was a bouquet of blood-red roses.

"We've spotted her," I whispered down to Kiev. "Just hold on a little longer…"

My words sent shivers running down my spine, despite the fact that he had Lilith's protective spell around him. Not only that, the black witches couldn't afford to harm him as long as they suspected him to be Magnus.

I reached instinctively for my waist, and then realized I'd discarded my clothes along with the dagger that I kept there. Kiev had no weapon, so I looked around at the others. "Do any of you have a dagger or any kind of weapon?" I asked.

Caleb was the first to reach into his belt and withdraw a knife. I lowered myself to him, took the blade and placed it on the ground so Kiev could pick it up. I looked my husband steadily in the eye. "You know what to do with it."

He nodded, clenching his jaw.

Checking the scene once again, Lilith had now reached the edge of the lake. Stretching out her arms, she levitated into the air and hovered over the center of it. My stomach churned as all of the witches surrounding her withdrew their knives from their sheaths. Each witch stood directly behind a human, the blades pointing downward, ready to strike as soon as the time was right.

I'd never witnessed a ritual quite like this. But I hoped that they planned to bring those daggers down later rather than sooner…

Once Lilith had stopped drifting upward, and it seemed that she had raised herself as high as she was going to, I exchanged glances with Kiev and nodded. I felt like a nervous wreck watching him leave us and clamber over the rocks.

Kiev had to put on the performance of his life. If Lilith got even the slightest clue that he was not Magnus, everything would come crashing down upon us, all of our efforts down the drain.

"Lilith." Magnus' voice boomed down upon the sacrificial area.

Lilith's eyes bulged in shock as her gaze shot toward Magnus standing on the rock. Her bouquet slipped from her hands and dropped into the lake. A deathly silence fell over the other witches as they all gazed at the vampire. Even

Rhys looked speechless, though it was hard to read that warlock's expression. I guessed his brain would soon start ticking over how to use Magnus' appearance to his advantage.

"Magnus?" Lilith gasped. "What you doing here?"

"I need to speak to you." Kiev held out a hand, indicating that she approach.

She glided away from the pool and landed on the rock where Kiev stood. Her lips parted as she continued staring at him in awe.

"How did you get here?"

Kiev's eyes darkened.

"What is wrong? Were you unable to escape on the boat?"

"I've woken from your spell," Kiev said, his voice steady and free from emotion.

"Spell?" Lilith asked. "What are you talking about?"

He reached up and grabbed Lilith's jaw. I had been afraid that the protection she had formed around him would prevent them from even touching. But it seemed that she was exempt.

Kiev nodded toward the lake, his eyes traveling over all the hogtied humans surrounding it. "I see now what drew you to me."

Lilith's face contorted with confusion.

"It made no sense to me at the time," Kiev continued,

"why you were so bent on pursuing a relationship with me even when the world you lived in forbade it. Why you made love to me so unhesitatingly behind your husband's back. Why you kept returning to me even at risk of destroying the reputation of your entire family… But now I understand. You knew what my immortality could do for you."

Lilith began shaking her head furiously. "No," she stammered. "No, Magnus. You have it all wrong." She reached out to grip his arms but he brushed her away, causing her to stumble backward.

"Had I been a warlock, you wouldn't have looked twice at me."

"It's not true, Magnus! I love you." She launched toward him again and gripped his hands, shaking him.

"Magnus!" Rhys boomed. "Get away from her."

When Kiev ignored him, he flew through the air toward him but, of course, he couldn't touch him. Besides, Lilith blasted him back with a spell.

"I have too many reasons to disbelieve you," Kiev said. "As far as I can see, every action of yours to date has led up to this ritual. From the moment we met, to allowing me to be kidnapped, dragging me from the life I'd managed to rebuild for myself, keeping me with you in your chamber for centuries so that you could stay alive… it's all been leading up to this point."

"I wouldn't be alive today if I didn't love you," she said, desperation in her voice. "I told you that already."

"Then we do not share the same definition of love."

She cast her eyes about at all the witches, waiting and staring up at her, then fixed her gaze on Magnus once more. "Then what do I have to do to prove it to you? Tell me!"

Kiev glanced down at the ceremonial setup. "Back out of this ritual."

Lilith's breath hitched.

"That's the only way you can prove it to me."

She gaped at the vampire. She glanced down at the pool, then back at Magnus. "Magnus, you don't understand—"

"I understand more than you think."

"I have to do this."

"Then you choose this ritual over me."

"It's not like that."

"Yes, witch. It is."

She bit down hard on her lower lip even as it trembled.

Silence followed as she stared down at her feet. Even though I felt crazy for it, I couldn't help but feel pity for the woman.

Although there was truth in Kiev's words, I couldn't deny that Lilith did love Magnus. She hadn't made the right choices in her life, but then neither had I for much of my own life. I'd had a glimpse for myself of what her upbringing had been like. It was hardly any wonder that she'd turned out the way she had. And yet she had found room for Magnus in her black heart. Even though Magnus was hardly a ray of sunshine, it seemed to me that to Lilith he had been a light in the darkness and evil that was her existence. I could only imagine the pain that Kiev was inflicting on her.

"Don't listen to him," Rhys had begun to shout. "Get away from him!"

Isolde and Julisse both tried to approach Lilith, but she blasted them back before they could come near.

Slowly, Lilith raised her gaze to Magnus once again. Her dark eyes were drowning in pain as she whispered, "I cannot choose you, my love. You don't understand... I was born for this."

"And I was born for *this*."

Whipping out Caleb's knife from his belt, Kiev plunged it right into her chest.

Shrieks abounded as all the witches and warlocks present hurtled toward Kiev in the air, only to be unable to pry him away from Lilith.

"For every evil born, another is born to counter it," Kiev hissed into Lilith's ear. "I'm not the man you thought I was. Raised by the enemies of your ancestors, I was designed to be your downfall... I played you at your own game, witch." He paused, watching as blood spilled from her mouth, her youthful appearance rapidly fading and turning corpselike before our very eyes.

Then Kiev spoke the last words her tortured soul would ever hear.

"I, Magnus Helios, never loved you."

She'll never know just how much of a lie that is.

CHAPTER 28: ROSE

I jumped as screaming erupted behind the rocks. It sounded like someone was being murdered. I prayed that someone was Lilith.

I looked toward my parents, raising my eyebrows. Then all eyes shot up toward Mona.

I wanted to call up to her, but she was too high up. I couldn't risk being heard. Corrine and Ibrahim lifted themselves into the air to see what was happening. Corrine gasped. Then they both lowered themselves down.

"What?" my father demanded, gripping Ibrahim's shoulders and shaking him.

"Lilith," he said. "Kiev did it."

Mona descended behind Ibrahim and Corrine, her skin

looking sallow.

"A rotten corpse," she said, her voice choked. "That's all that's left of her. The last Ancient among us."

"Where is Kiev?" Helina asked, her eyes lit with panic.

"Guys," Aiden said suddenly. "Look."

We all spun round to face him. He had stepped within the boundary.

It seemed that with Lilith, the boundary had vanished too. We all hurried forward and were able to enter as though no barrier had ever existed.

There was a wheezing sound behind me. I turned in time to see Mona falling to her knees on the sharp rocks, bent over double. My mother and Matteo rushed to her, laying her down gently on the ground as she seemed to lose control of her limbs. Her eyes drooped and shut.

Corrine hurried over too and bent down, touching her forehead.

"What's going on?" I asked.

"I have no idea," Corrine said.

Matteo, Erik and Helina pushed through, squatting next to Corrine and peering down at Mona.

"It must have something to do with Lilith's death," Erik said. "Mona's powers were dependent on her."

"She's blacked out," Corrine said.

I backed away from the crowd huddled around Mona and, cupping my palms, dipped them in the waves. Then I rushed back to the unconscious witch and tipped the water over her. That didn't help.

"Ibrahim, Corrine," Matteo urged. "Do something."

The witch and warlock began working their magic, even as the uproar on the other side of the rock increased.

"It's Mag—Kiev," Micah called behind us.

A moment later, Kiev, still in Magnus' form, dropped down from the rocks above. His right shoulder looked badly burned.

"Mona!" He threw himself to the ground next to his wife, gripping her head between his hands. "What happened?"

"Hush," Corrine said. "We're trying to revive her."

"We don't have time for that," Caleb muttered. I looked up at where he was pointing.

A line of witches had appeared above the rocks and spotted us. Kiev didn't allow Corrine and Ibrahim to attempt to finish their cure. He grabbed Mona and began running in the opposite direction. The black witches' spells began to hurtle down toward us, bouncing off the rocks and hitting in all directions. The mayhem found me separated from everyone as I dodged to avoid a curse. When one ricocheted so close to me it singed my right ear, I spun around to find myself face to face with Isolde.

Her eyes glinted with mad fury, her chest heaving. She was too close for me to dodge her curse as it hurtled right for my chest. The force of it knocked me backward and winded me completely. My head slammed against a rock. It was all I could do to not lose consciousness.

No.

My story does not end here.

Not at the hands of this bitch.

Even as my skin felt like hot oil had just been poured over it and the sensation began to spread across my chest and down my arms, I gritted my teeth and forced myself to stand. She was approaching me, a look of triumph on her face. She raised her palms, motioning to strike again.

Summoning the fire within me, I forced flames from my palms. Her eyes widened with shock as they engulfed her.

I expected her to shoot out a spell to extinguish my flames but, bizarrely, she didn't. She just began screaming as though she really was being burned.

I gaped at the witch as she stumbled around on the rocks. She was too disorientated even to make it to the sea. This was not the Isolde that I had come to know.

"Rose! Are you all right?" Mona called behind me. I was surprised to see her making her way toward me with Kiev. She was paler than I'd ever seen her, but her legs seemed steady.

The three of us stood watching in awe as Isolde burned alive until her screams subsided and her body stopped moving. She collapsed to the ground as a lump of melted flesh and bone. I shuddered, watching the flames lick at her corpse.

Mona grabbed my shoulders and twisted me to face her. Her face dropped as she stared at my chest and looked along my shoulders and arms. I looked down at myself for the first time. My skin was tinged red, but truly, the pain had felt much worse than it looked. It barely looked more serious than nettle stings. The pain was also subsiding.

"You should be dead," Mona breathed as she continued looking me over. "Isolde wouldn't have hit you with anything other than one of her most deadly curses. And her powers were practically on par with Rhys'." Then she addressed her husband, whom I still hadn't gotten used to looking like Magnus. "My blackout and now this… I and all the black witches… we have become weak. Our spells no longer hold the potency they once did. It's because Lilith is gone. The spell she cast on you has also disappeared."

"At least this is confirmation that she is definitely gone," I muttered, "and she's not somehow still hanging on in that rotten body of hers."

My voice trailed off as the three of us looked around the rocky area. The smoke from my fire was thinning and we could see more clearly. Everyone had moved on from the area—over the rocks and further toward the castle, by the sound of it. It was just Kiev, Mona and me left here now.

We started moving to join the battle that was taking place near the castle, but Mona stopped in her tracks as we passed Isolde's ashes. She levitated them off the ground, floated them toward the ocean and scattered them in the waves.

"She would never have done that for you. Why would you do that?" Kiev asked, looking at her in surprise.

"Because, Kiev, I've chosen to be a better person than Isolde was," Mona replied, watching the remainder of the ashes sink beneath the surface. "And, after death, I believe everyone deserves at least some respect."

Chapter 29: Rose

We reached the rocks and climbed over them, now in full view of the battle. Curses flew in all directions as vampires and witches clashed. Corrine and Ibrahim were taking on several witches at once which, to my surprise, they seemed to be coping quite well with. A single curse from Ibrahim floored three witches in his path.

"White witches are now more powerful than black witches," I muttered, more to myself than to anyone else.

"Lilith's demise has drained us," Mona said.

"You think you were the only one who fainted?" I asked.

"No. I'm sure that most of these black witches passed out at least for a short while... depending on how much power they gained from Lilith. Channelers like me would have felt it the most. Can either of you see Rhys?" Mona asked.

Kiev and I shook our heads. I wasn't sure whether that was a good thing or bad thing.

I tried to make out my family and Caleb, but it was hard to spot vampires in this darkness—most of them were moving so fast in the churning crowd.

"Let's go," Kiev said impatiently.

Leaving our hiding place, we rushed down the rocks toward the battleground. I took a different direction than the couple, my palms at the ready to begin blasting fire at these black witches who had taken so many innocent lives. Adrenaline rushed through me, and there wasn't the slightest bit of mercy running through my veins.

I was about to throw myself headfirst into the battle when I caught a glimpse to my right of a vat of deep red liquid. It was so large, a lake would have been a better word to describe it. Surrounding it were humans, and I realized that many of the screams and cries were coming from them. Before I could help with the battle, I had to do something about them. Spells were inching dangerously close to them and they were helpless. They could barely wriggle a few feet.

As I approached the lake, I spotted my mother and Ashley on the other side of it. They had already started freeing the humans, ripping through the ropes with their fangs. I rushed over to them and began working alongside them. I didn't have any knife or sharp object on me. I did, however, have my palms. I approached a girl nearest to me, who looked older than me.

"It's okay," I said as she squealed. "I'm here to help."

She was writhing so much that I was afraid she might fall right into the pond and drown, being unable to swim to the surface.

Gripping the rope that bound her ankles and wrists together, I tried to move her gently toward me, away from the edge of the lake, before placing both palms around the rope and sending heat surging through it. I had to be careful not to send through too much in case I lit the whole rope on fire and ended up burning her. I managed to release just enough to singe the rope and make it weak enough so that it snapped.

The girl stretched out her limbs for the first time in God knew how long. Tears of relief filled her eyes as I helped her to sit up. I wanted to stay with her for a moment longer to comfort her that the worst was over, but there were too many other humans waiting for me to attend to. Even with Ashley, my mother and me working, we still had a mammoth task ahead of us.

"We need to hurry," my mother said, eyeing the humans still bound.

After the first girl I'd released, the others were faster. I was beginning to feel more confident with my heat so close to their bodies, and I was able to singe through the ropes much faster.

As we released the humans, we ordered those who were able to stand on their weak legs to hide round the side of the castle where nobody seemed to be right now. Once there was a substantial crowd waiting there, my mother told Ashley to wait with them.

I wiped sweat from my brow, looking over our progress. We had about three dozen left. It was still a lot, but nothing compared to how many there had been when we had first started.

"No!" A shrill voice pierced my eardrums. It sounded no further than twenty feet away. I was in the middle of bending over a girl and turned in time to see Julisse racing full speed toward me. Her dark curly hair was scattered across her sweaty face, her eyes practically red with rage.

I tried to shoot flames at her, but she had managed to conjure up a shield of water around herself with whatever power she had left in her.

I braced myself for impact, expecting to fall back into the lake of blood, when something raced past me in a blur. The next thing I knew, Julisse crashed to the ground, Caleb on top of her. She struggled beneath him, but Caleb was too quick. Before she could summon a curse, he'd already slashed through both of her palms. Then, lowering his head to her neck, he sank his fangs deep into her flesh and jerked upward, ripping right through her jugular.

Blood spurted everywhere, soaking the ground and forming a pool quickly. Finally, extending his nails as far as they would go, he severed her head completely. It rolled around sickeningly on the ground before halting in the middle of the pool of blood, face down.

Caleb got off her still-twitching body and when he turned to face me, he looked more menacing than I had ever seen him before. His chest heaved, his mouth dripping with blood, his eyes much darker.

Wow. Go Caleb.

His gaze sent shivers running through me. I was so used to him being gentle with me, I often forgot just how ferocious he could be. He wiped away the blood from his mouth with the back of his hand and then, since he was already shirtless, he tore a piece of fabric from the hem of Julisse' dress and wiped his hands on it.

He walked toward me, his eyes warming a little as he looked down at me. He examined my skin, which was still red from the curse that Isolde had shot at me.

"Are you okay?" he asked.

"Yeah," I said. "You?"

He nodded. His skin was also tinged red. Clearly he had survived a curse like I had—more confirmation of Mona's statement that the black witches had lost their touch.

I didn't spend much time with Caleb before he left me and raced back into the battle. I needed to finish helping my mother free the rest of the humans. We worked quickly, and luckily no more distractions came before we finished releasing all of them. We herded those who could walk around the side of the castle toward Ashley, then came back to assist those who couldn't stand. Many were just in shock, while others had genuine injuries.

Once we had finished, we left Ashley with them and cautiously approached the battle again. It was still raging, though, as before, we seemed to have the upper hand. Ibrahim and Corrine hadn't let up their efforts. I scanned the area for my father. He stood near my grandfather, back to back as they clashed with four warlocks.

My stomach felt queasy as I caught sight of Micah— now in his werewolf form since nightfall had already arrived—biting off the hands of a screaming witch with his huge jaws. I looked around for Mona, wondering where she'd gotten to. I couldn't see her anywhere. For that matter, I still couldn't spot Rhys either.

I was about to suggest to my mother that we start helping when a thought struck me. "I wonder if there are more humans in the castle?"

"Let's check," my mother replied.

We didn't want to be distracted by anyone attacking us, so we made our way as discreetly as possible around the edge of the battleground toward the main entrance of the castle. I looked at my mother just before we entered. I wasn't sure what surprises this house of horrors held for us this time, but I didn't think it wise for the two of us to go alone.

"I think we should take at least one other person with us," I said.

"I'll come." A gruff voice came from behind us. It was Micah—now finished with the witch he'd been mauling. He had blood smeared on his mouth as he looked up at us, his eyes gleaming.

"Okay," I said.

A vampire, a werewolf and a fire-wielder. It felt like we'd make a decent team.

We pushed open the entrance doors and stepped inside, closing them behind us. I hoped that nobody had seen us enter. With the doors shut, it was eerily quiet. We stood still, listening and looking around the grand entry hall for any sign of life.

"You hear or smell anything?" I asked Micah and my mother.

They both shook their heads.

"No human blood?"

"No," Micah said.

"If Micah can't smell it, I doubt we'll have much luck," my mother said. "But we're here now. Let's check anyway."

"We should check the dungeon first," Micah said.

We headed toward the kitchen and forced open the trap door. As we descended the steps, a sickly stench engulfed us. We cast our eyes around at the empty cells, moving from one room to another. But we spotted no humans, or any other creature for that matter. The dungeons were empty.

"Let's check upstairs now," I said.

We exited the dungeons, passed through the kitchen and headed to the wide staircase leading up to the first level. I felt so jittery, I jumped even at the creak of a floorboard beneath our feet.

My mother held my hand, supporting me as we climbed. It was dark and except for the occasional lantern, I was relying on the moonlight trickling through the windows to see where I was going.

Reaching the first level, we hurried along the corridor, checking in each room as we passed by—at least all the rooms whose doors opened. We climbed level after level, meeting nothing but more silence. Finally, we reached the level of the spell room and stopped outside its deep red door. I stared at it, then slowly reached out and hovered my hand over the handle. The three of us pressed our ears against the wood, listening for any sign of life.

There was nothing.

"Now that Lilith is gone," I whispered, "if we opened

this door and stepped inside, I wonder if we would be doomed?"

Micah shrugged. "I don't know. But it's not worth the risk. If there was anyone in there, I would sure as hell know it by now."

And so he retreated from the door. We searched the rest of the floor and then the few levels above, followed by the roof. I pointed to the cage at the far end of the roof. "That was the cage I freed Hermia and her friends from."

"And it's a good thing you did," my mother said.

Micah grunted as we left the roof and made our way back down the stairs. "I would have just left them there."

Reaching the next level down, we stopped and looked at each other. It was time to concede defeat. There were no humans in this castle. There was so much blood in that lake, it was no wonder that it was empty.

We made our way quickly down to the ground floor again. Ten steps away from the second level, my mother and Micah stopped suddenly. My mother gripped my arm, pulling me back.

"What is it?" I asked.

My question was answered by a deep growl. It came from the bottom of the staircase. Straining to see through the darkness, I could make out a pair of gleaming red eyes and white teeth, shiny with saliva.

Oh, great. Not another one of Shadow's siblings.

My mother shoved me behind her, extending her claws and preparing to approach it. But Micah brushed her aside with his head.

"Allow me," he growled, fixing his eyes on the dog.

Although the vampire dog was enormous, Micah was still larger, his jaws wider. The two animals launched at each other and clashed in the air. They attacked each other so ferociously they were a blur before my eyes. But when the vampire dog let out a deafening howl, it was clear that Micah had won. They stopped moving so fast and I could make out that Micah had closed his jaws around the dog's throat. Blood streamed down the sides of his mouth as he clamped down hard.

The vampire dog fell to the floor and writhed around as Micah lowered his mouth to the beast's chest. He mauled through its skin before finally closing his teeth around the dog's heart. He pulled out the giant organ and threw it down on the floor. I looked away, my stomach queasy. Even my mother couldn't stand the sight.

"Let's continue, shall we?" Micah called down from below.

Keeping my eyes firmly away from the mess that was left of the dog, we hurried past it toward the werewolf.

"You are gross, Micah," I muttered.

"Thanks," he said, licking his lips with his long tongue and grinning darkly.

We finished descending the staircases and reached the entry hall. Approaching the main entrance, my mother pushed open the doors slightly and peered out.

She looked back and nodded. "Let's go."

We stepped outside. Looking out at the battleground, I was pleasantly surprised by how few black witches remained. There were many bodies strewn around on the ground—none of our people, to my relief—and those who remained standing were badly injured and clearly on their last legs.

Aiden spotted us, having just finished slitting the throat of a witch, and approached.

"We're almost done here," he said calmly, looking over the area. "A lot of witches fled. They're shadows of their former selves."

I noticed that he had reddish skin like me. So did many of the other vampires that I could see. Although curses were hitting our people, they didn't seem to be having any serious effects other than causing pain.

My attention was drawn to a billow of flames my father had just shot out. Our vampires, along with Corrine and Ibrahim, seemed to be working together to force the remaining witches into a circle where my father could scorch them all at once. The remaining black witches, obviously realizing what was happening, vanished.

"Is that the last of them?" my mother asked.

"From what we can see," my father replied.

"What about Rhys?" Micah asked.

Aiden shook his head. "I haven't seen him."

Then Magnus—Kiev—called out: "Has anyone seen Mona?"

CHAPTER 30: MONA

As I raced with Kiev down from the rocks, the only person on my mind was Rhys. Wanting to avoid clashing with any other witch or warlock, I dodged in and out of the battle in search of him. When I had been watching the scene from the air as Kiev stabbed Lilith, the warlock had been near the pool. But I could see from where I was standing that he was not there now.

I suspected that he might have blacked out somewhere. He'd been the most dependent on Lilith for his powers of all of us—more than me, Julisse or even Isolde—so it would be no surprise if he was still unconscious. I wanted to find him before he came to.

Finally, I did. A long form cast in shadow lay close to

one side of the castle. He was lying flat on his back, his pale face set in a deep frown.

When I first laid eyes on him, I wondered for a moment whether he was even still living. But it soon became apparent to me that he was. His lips were parted and he breathed gently.

I bent down over him and touched his forehead. It wouldn't be difficult to finish him off now if I wanted to. I didn't even need to use magic. I could just reach for the knife tucked into my belt that I'd retrieved from Kiev.

But I couldn't bring myself to. I'd already experienced the aftermath of self-disgust that came with killing a person in their sleep. I wasn't about to do it again—not even with Rhys.

Keeping my fingers against his skin, I surged energy into his body and jolted him awake.

His eyelids flickered open and he sat up. He looked shocked as he pushed himself back away from me and shot to his feet.

I took in the deep lines in his face. The dark shadows beneath his eyes. The sallowness of his skin. He looked nothing like the man I had known only months ago.

I couldn't even bring myself to feel anger toward him. All I felt was sadness, and a sense of loss for the life he could have chosen.

When he motioned to raise his arms, I shook my head.

"Let's not end things like this, Rhys. The game is over. Just give it up."

My words only seemed to aggravate him as he took a step closer to me and grabbed my jaw.

I didn't flinch as he glared down at me, nor even when heat started surging through his hand into my body.

"Please," I said. "Stop." I reached a hand up to his face. He flinched at my touch, then tightened his grip around me and pinned me against the castle wall, his hands moving down to my throat.

"I know what you did," I choked. Even though I knew he could snap my neck with the strength of his muscles alone, I still refused to feel intimidated by him. "Back in The Shade... you saved me from the fire, didn't you? How else would I have ended up on a boat in the middle of a lake?"

His eyes narrowed. But he refused to answer my question. Instead, he let go of me and blasted me backward with a spell. I found myself falling from the battleground and landing on the rocks beneath. Fortunately, the rocks my back hit were partially submerged in the water and had sea flora growing over them, which helped to soften the impact.

Groaning, I forced myself to sit up.

Okay, then. If this is how you want to play it...

As soon as I caught sight of him appearing on the rocks

above me, I cast a spell that knocked him from his feet and brought him crashing down on the ground a short distance from me.

He climbed to his feet, blood flowing from a cut in his lower lip.

"What do you have to gain by continuing to fight us?" I said. "Where do you go from here? Take a look at yourself in a mirror, for God's sake. You look like a ghost."

I narrowly dodged another spell from him before shooting one at him myself. With each spell that I let loose, my body felt weaker and weaker. The lack of strength was alarming. I was used to being so powerful I could take on a dozen white witches at once. Now I doubted that I would even be able to take on Corrine alone.

As we continued to blast each other with spells, it became apparent that he too was feeling the strain. His curses were beginning to do less damage each time one hit me. Finally, the spells that hit me barely caused more discomfort than a prickle.

Realizing the futility of attacking me with spells, he reached for his belt and pulled out a ceremonial dagger, the same one I'd seen him holding earlier before the ritual. Even as we circled each other, I couldn't help but notice how strange it was. Rhys and I, among the most powerful witches of our time, were now fighting with less grace than even vampires.

I could see the shame of it in Rhys' eyes. The humiliation. I knew the pride he took in his magic—it was the only thing he lived for. He had always chosen it over me, even when he'd claimed to love me. He loved magic even more than he loved himself.

I didn't stand a chance against him physically. He was taller, stronger and more skilled in combat. The only thing that had made the match even slightly fair before was the fact that I could wield magic.

Still, I wasn't going to run from him.

This was a battle I had to fight alone.

As he closed in on me, I wondered whether he had it in him to kill me this time. Although he wouldn't admit to it, I knew he'd saved me from the burning tree. And that day when he and his army had attacked The Shade, he'd avoided killing me then even though it would have been easy. He'd had me tied up in a tree. He could have done anything he wanted to me. But he hadn't.

Rhys lurched forward. It was almost embarrassing how easily he wrestled the knife out of my hand and pinned me to the ground. My back flat against a rock, I stared up into his black eyes.

His blade pressed against my neck.

My skin broke.

A trickle of blood ran down my neck.

I've pushed him too far.

He's going to do it.

Regret consumed me as he pushed the blade even harder against my flesh. *How could I have been so selfish? I have more than just myself to think about. Kiev is half of me.*

I should have just run...

I began to struggle harder against him.

He lifted himself off me abruptly.

I thought for a moment that I'd managed to kick him in a painful place, but he was showing no signs of pain as he stood over me. Looking down at me through hooded eyelids, he raised his dagger again. Fearing he was about to hurl it through my chest, I rolled over on my side.

But I didn't need to.

He brought the dagger down against his right wrist, then his left, slashing through his arteries.

Casting one last, lingering glance down at me, he displayed raw emotions for the first time. Frustration. Longing. Perhaps even regret.

Then our gaze was ripped apart as he leapt across the rocks and dove into the ocean.

Breathless, I scrambled to my feet and hurried to the spot where he had just disappeared. The waves were tinged red with his blood. But he was showing no sign of surfacing.

This part of the ocean was teeming with sharks. It would not be long before they claimed him.

Despite myself, tears welled in my eyes and spilled down my cheeks. My vision blurred as I stared at the churning water.

And so it ends.

The life of a man who could have had everything, yet in the end chose nothing.

Goodbye, old friend.

Chapter 31: Rose

"There she is!" I shouted as Mona clambered over the rocks toward us. She looked exhausted, cuts and bruises covering her body.

Kiev was the first to rush over to her. "What happened to you? Are you okay?"

I was surprised to see that her eyes were watery. She swallowed hard. "I'm fine."

"Have you seen Rhys?"

"Yes," she said. "We… will not be seeing him again."

"He's dead?" I asked, gaping at her.

"Yes. He took his own life."

We all fell into hushed silence.

"I always knew there was a screw missing with him,"

Micah said after several moments.

Mona bit her lip, a pained expression on her face. "There was something missing, that's for sure."

"So," my mother said. "Now what? Ashley is still waiting around the side of the castle with the humans we managed to free. Some of them are in a bad state. They need medical attention."

We all looked around the battleground, scorched from my father's flames and strewn with blood and bodies.

What we had just accomplished still hadn't sunk in. We'd spent so long fighting to end these enemies and thwart their various plans, for it to come to an end... it seemed surreal.

"There is a gate within this castle, as most of you should know," Mona said. "We can travel through it back to the human realm."

I exchanged a glance with Caleb. "Uh," he began, "I'm not sure that will work."

"Why not?" Mona asked.

"When a group of us came here to rescue humans days ago, we destroyed the other side of the castle. Or rather, the dragons did. If we pass through the gate, we'll meet a colossal pile of rubble."

Mona turned to Corrine and Ibrahim. "Why don't the two of you go through and clear out a path? I'm sure you could manage that."

Ibrahim raised a brow. "We're talking about an entire collapsed castle. Yes, I'm sure Corrine and I can create a path through to the surface, but it will take time."

"That's fine," Mona said calmly. "I still have some unfinished business."

"What's that?" my father asked.

Mona glanced at Kiev. "Magnus," she replied. "I left him at the bottom of a river. I need to go free him." Then her deep blue eyes turned on me. "Rose, I would like you to accompany me. If their boundary is back up, there's no way I'd be able to blast through in this weak state. The witches of The Sanctuary have many reasons to dislike me, so I can't even be sure they'd let me in if I went alone. You, on the other hand, have their respect."

"Okay," I said.

"Ibrahim and I will get started then," Corrine said, catching her husband's hand and walking with him toward the entrance of the castle.

I embraced Caleb, and then hugged my parents and grandfather, before catching Mona's arm. I had grown so used to being transported places with magic by now, it felt as normal for me to hurtle through the air at lightning speed as it was for a human to hop on a bus.

The battleground disappeared and a few seconds later, Mona and I were standing alone on a beautiful beach outside The Sanctuary.

"So we're going to have to attract someone's attention again," I said.

"Yeah," Mona said, already looking toward the boundary.

As we neared the trees lining the beach, it was clear that we would not have nearly as much trouble this time. I guessed because of the black witches breaking in, more witches and warlocks were on guard. Within a matter of seconds I'd already spotted a warlock prowling around in the forest. A young, handsome warlock with long blond hair.

"Hey! Over here!" Mona shouted.

He stopped in his tracks and made his way toward us.

As he drew within ten feet, Mona spun around, her back to him. Her face had turned bright red. "Oh, no," she said beneath her breath. "I know this guy. Coen Brymer. Talk to him for me, will you?"

I agreed but it was already too late. Coen Brymer had recognized Mona.

"Hey, Mona," Coen said. "Whatever happened to you?"

Sighing deeply, Mona turned around to face him even as she avoided eye contact. "I'm sorry, Coen. I don't have time to talk. Will you just let us inside, please?"

He looked at me. "Who is your companion?"

"Rose Novak," I answered. "Please let us inside now. I have an understanding with—"

"Oh, yes, I know," he said quickly. "Hermia informed us about the agreement she made with you. You are welcome and since Mona is with you, I can only assume she's welcome too."

He stepped through the boundary and held out both arms for Mona and I to take before leading us back inside.

"Might your visit to The Sanctuary be long enough to take a stroll with me by the waterfall?" Coen asked Mona.

Mona gave him a weak smile, then raised her ring finger to him. "I doubt it, Coen. But I wish you the best of luck in finding happiness."

I couldn't miss the disappointment in his face as he eyed her ring. But then he covered it up with another smile. "Congratulations, and thank you."

Mona didn't hang around for more small talk. She held my hand and vanished us again. This time, we reappeared at the bank of the river. There was nobody in sight, just lush forest.

Mona left my side and began wading into the water. I was about to follow after her when she turned around. "Just wait there."

I did as she had requested, watching as she disappeared beneath the churning waters. As promised, she surfaced less than a minute later. Bobbing in the water by her side was Magnus. His whole body was rigid, though I could detect the fury behind his eyes.

"You can help me now, Rose," she said. I hurried forward and caught his right arm while Mona gripped his left. Together, we dragged him onto the bank.

"He doesn't look, uh, too happy," I said, looking down at him with concern. "Were you planning to just release your spell from him while we're standing here?"

"You have a point," she said.

We both chewed on our lower lips as we looked back down to him.

"I have an idea," Mona said. "Let's take him to the beach."

"Which beach?" I asked.

"You'll see," she said.

Holding onto us, she transported us outside of the boundary to a beach I'd never visited before. Looking out toward the ocean, I spotted a boat. It was small yet sturdy-looking, and it had a roof.

When I looked down at the vampire again, if anything, the anger in his eyes had increased at our delay.

"I think you'd better just release him now," I said. "I guess that boat is for him?"

Mona nodded, looking toward the boat, an unexpected look of melancholy in her eyes.

"I guess you'll vanish us immediately so he doesn't have a chance to attack?" I said.

Mona paused, biting her lip again, still looking down at

the vampire.

"You run further up the beach in case he decides to," Mona said. "I need to speak to him. And I don't feel comfortable speaking to him while keeping him like this. I'm going to release him… I doubt he'll attack."

I sighed. "Well, in that case I will stay with you. I'm probably better equipped to fight him with my fire power than you in your current state."

"You're right," she muttered.

She bent down on her knees over Magnus and touched his forehead. My hands grew sweaty as the witch muttered some words and Magnus regained control of his body. His limbs stretched out and he shot to his feet. His chiseled face took on a look of utter aggravation.

"Why the hell did you do that?" he growled at Mona. "If you weren't a woman, I would grab your throat and maul you."

Mona took a step back from his rage. "I'm sorry, Magnus. I had my reasons for doing it. But you are free now. Nobody will bother you again. Not any of the black witches, not me, or any of the white witches."

"Where is Lilith?" he asked, his brows furrowing and causing a deep line in the center of his forehead.

Mona's voice caught in her throat. "She… passed away."

Magnus's eyes narrowed, as though he could hardly believe her words.

"That boat you see," Mona said, her voice unsteady. "Lilith arranged that for you so that you could escape safely, and continue with your life… with whomever you choose to spend it with. I wouldn't be surprised if you even find blood bags in there."

"I don't understand."

"She chose to spend the last hours of her life with you, Magnus. That's all you need to understand. And what I said before about her using you was not fair. She did love you. Madly. Deeply. At least as deeply as her heart could manage. And she wanted you to know that before she passed away. You may not have realized it, but for all those years… you held her heart in your hand."

Magnus was speechless. I could've sworn that I saw the corners of his eyes moisten as he turned and looked toward the boat floating in the ocean.

None of us spoke a word for the next few minutes.

Finally he faced Mona again, clearing his throat. "Thank you for confirming what I… sometimes doubted. It means a lot to me." His voice was deeper than it had been a few minutes ago.

His eyes traveled from me to Mona one last time before he turned his back on us and entered the waves, wading toward the boat. Mona and I stood in silence, watching as he boarded it, settled himself in and began sailing away into the brightening horizon toward God knew where.

I didn't care… As long as we never had to go searching for the guy again.

Chapter 32: Rose

When Mona and I arrived back at the black witches' island, nobody was outside. We headed straight to the castle, walked through the entrance hall and found everyone had gathered in the kitchen. They all looked toward us as we entered.

"Well?" Kiev asked, Magnus' face lighting up.

"I set him free," Mona said.

"Good," he replied. "And... Do you have any idea when I will turn back into myself?"

A smile crossed Mona's lips. She exchanged a glance with my mother. "I, um... I think we can probably expect within a few days. I pulled a hair from his head, you see."

"How are Ibrahim and Corrine progressing?" I asked.

"They are down there now, still working," my father replied.

"Do you know how long they will be?" I asked.

"Hopefully not much more than ten minutes. They have made quite a lot of progress already, or so they say. None of us have been down there. But Corrine has come back up to keep us updated."

I looked toward the open trap door and moved toward it, poking my head down. I caught sight of the gate. Landis and Ashley stood next to it, and all of the humans were already down there. Most of them were resting against the wall, looking exhausted. I noted that those who were injured had not been treated yet. Ibrahim and Corrine had been in a hurry to start work on clearing out a trail. None of the injuries looked fatal, so I hoped that they would be all right. We would find some time to treat them once we reached the other side.

Someone touched my back, and I turned to see Caleb.

"Come with me," he whispered into my ear.

Before I could respond, he twined his fingers with mine and pulled me through the exit of the kitchen, out of view from everyone.

Placing his hands either side of my waist, he pressed me back gently against the wall. His lips met mine. He reached his hands up to my cheeks, caressing them as he kissed me tenderly.

When he drew away, he was staring at me intently, his dark hair touching the sides of his face. His seriousness amused me.

"What was that about?" I asked.

He gave me a small smile. "Since when do I need a reason to kiss my bride?"

My bride. The words made my spine tingle.

I reached my arms around his neck and pulled him down for another long, slow kiss. "Since never," I whispered.

His cool lips began trailing down my neck, soothing my irritated skin.

Our moment was interrupted by Micah. "Come on, you love birds," he growled. "Ibrahim and Corrine are finished earlier than expected."

I was annoyed at the interruption, but I was also relieved that we could finally get away from this place. I detached myself from Caleb and we followed Micah back into the kitchen. Everyone was already beginning to pile down into the dungeon. Caleb was the last to enter the dungeon. He shut the trap door behind him.

"I wonder if this will be the last time that anyone sets foot in this place," I said.

Caleb shrugged.

"I'll go down first," my father said, nearing the edge of the gate.

"Corrine definitely said that it was safe to go through now?" I asked.

"Yes," he replied. "I suggest you all send the humans down after me, and the rest of you follow after them."

With that, my father leapt through. I turned to the humans—mostly young women—lined up along the wall.

I smiled kindly. "Come on, guys."

"Where are you taking us?" one of them asked, her voice nervous.

"Back home. You're all from California, aren't you?" That seemed to be where the black witches had been targeting the most intensely—at least, according to the news.

"I am," she said.

"What about the rest of you?" I asked, addressing the others.

"Yes," they all confirmed.

"That certainly makes things easier for us," my mother said.

"What is that thing?" several of the girls asked as they neared the starry crater.

"It's a... uh..." *How do I even explain?* "It's a tunnel that will take you back home," was the best and fastest way I could think to answer them.

Several more questions were asked, but we didn't have time to answer them.

The girl who had volunteered to step toward first stared down at the seemingly endless abyss.

"Won't I die if I jump down there?"

"You'll be fine," I said. "My father is waiting for you at the other end."

"Okay," she said, though she sounded anything but okay.

Closing her eyes, she leaped through, her screams trailing behind her as she catapulted downward. I admired her bravery. To be so trusting of a complete stranger... Then again, they were desperate.

"Who's next?" my mother called.

Another girl inched forward and took the leap. One after another, we finished piling in the humans before the rest of us lined up to jump through. Caleb and I hung back. Holding hands, we dropped through together.

Before the roof of the dungeon could disappear completely, I glanced up at it for the last time.

So long, creepy castle.

***

On reaching the end of the tunnel, Caleb and I landed on the floor. I managed to land on all fours so as to avoid injuring my back. I'd learned that from experience.

Caleb was already standing by the time I looked at him. He reached out a hand and helped me up. Everyone else was also standing. The humans looked shaken, but they seemed to be okay. Even the injured ones whom we'd had to pick up and drop through seemed to have landed without too much added injury.

"Through here," my father said, pointing to the open trap door in the ceiling above us. A staircase led up to it, and beyond was a round hole that Ibrahim and Corrine had carved through the rubble. A ladder made of rope dangled through it, its bottom touching the top of the stairs. My father climbed up first, and then indicated that we follow. Again, we helped humans up, and those humans who couldn't climb due to injuries hung onto the backs of vampires.

To say that Micah had some trouble getting through was an understatement. Aside from the fact that wolves were hardly equipped to climb vertically up a rope ladder, his body was just so wide. It was a struggle for even Ibrahim and Corrine to levitate him through the hole, but with much complaining from Micah, they managed it eventually.

Climbing up through the hole with Caleb, I was struck instantly by the temperature. I'd been expecting to be hit by a wave of cold. Instead a mild breeze wafted toward us. Reaching the top, we found ourselves standing among the sprawling ruins of the castle, beyond which the trees were no longer coated with a sheet of white. For as far as I could see, there were gorgeous forests. The fresh smell of pine filled the air, and I even heard the chirping of early-morning birds.

"The curse has lifted," Caleb said quietly as he took in the scene along with me.

I had not been able to appreciate the beauty of the island before, because it had all looked the same. But now, with life finally bursting through after God knew how many decades, or even centuries, I realized just how breathtaking this place was.

The landscape was beginning to brighten from the first signs of the sun approaching beneath the horizon. I could only imagine how stunning this place would look in full sunshine.

Who would've thought…

I breathed in deeply, relishing the fresh warm air. Caleb's arm wrapped around me, pulling me closer. I rested my head against his chest as we continued admiring the island that had once been a prison to both of us.

Although this island had held many horrors for me, it would always hold a special place in my heart. It'd been where the seeds of my feelings for Caleb had first developed. I remembered how he'd kept me locked in that apartment, refusing to let me out or even speak to me. Thinking back on it now, I smiled, finding humor in the situation.

I nestled my head closer against my fiancé and raised my gaze to his face. His expression was calm, peaceful. Sensing me watching him, he grazed his lips over my forehead.

Perhaps one day, Caleb and I will return to this island with our children, stand in this very spot, and recount our story to them like old fogeys.

CHAPTER 33: ROSE

Now that we were back in the human realm, Corrine and Ibrahim took time to treat all those humans who were injured. I was beginning to feel tense at how much time they were taking. It wouldn't be long now until the sun rose, and made things much more difficult for our vampires.

"How much longer?" my father asked, sharing my tenseness.

"Just give us one more minute," Corrine said. "This is the last girl I'm treating. The rest are fine to walk and can be treated in a hospital when they return."

It ended up taking her five more minutes, but eventually, all the humans were able to stand, which was the most important thing for now.

"All right," Ibrahim said, looking over everyone. "Form a circle and make sure you're all touching."

"You know we need to head to California?" my mother asked, looking toward Ibrahim and Corrine.

"Yes," Corrine said. "Any beach along California will do… We just need to get in touch with the police and they will take things from there."

We all formed a circle and the witches transported us to a quiet beach. Relief spread across the humans' faces.

"Hey," one of the girls piped up. "My house is just round the corner from here."

"You can return home if you want," my mother said, "if you're sure you'll be okay."

The girl nodded eagerly. "I've no idea who the heck you people are—or if I can even call you people—but thank you for saving us," she gushed, and turned on her heel, hurrying away toward the road.

"If anyone else recognizes the area you are also free to go," my mother said.

Nobody else responded.

"Okay," Corrine said. "The rest of you will be left with the police. They'll take care of you."

"Mom, Dad, do either of you recognize this area?" I asked.

They looked around, then shook their heads. "Our

house wasn't near here," my mother replied.

"So if we don't know the location of any police station," I said, "we'll have to find a telephone."

"Rose, Sofia and I can escort them," my father said. "There's no need for all of us to come. The rest of you just wait here for us." He glanced toward the horizon. "We'll be as quick as possible."

With that, the three of us set off with the humans toward the road. There were hardly any cars around at this early hour.

"If any of you spot a phone booth, let us know," my mother said.

We walked along the sidewalk for the next ten minutes. Our pace was frustratingly slow. I just wasn't used to traveling at regular human speed any more.

Finally, one of the girls called out. "Look, there's one on the other side."

We crossed the road and approached the booth. My father picked up the phone, dialed 911 and turned to my mother and me as he held the phone to his ear.

"Check the name of this road," he said.

My mother and I stepped away, located a signpost and noted the name.

After the call had connected, we gave my father the details he needed. Less than a minute later, he was done talking and replaced the phone.

"They're coming for you," he said, looking around at the humans.

They positively beamed.

"Rose, Sofia," he said, "We'll wait on the other side of the road, behind those bushes, until the police arrive—just to make sure they get picked up okay."

"Good idea," I said. There was no point in waiting here in full view of the police or they'd just entangle us in questions.

"Where do you live?" one of the girls asked, eyeing my father.

The three of us exchanged glances. "Not in California," was all the answer she received from him.

We said goodbye to the humans and then ducked down behind the bushes on the opposite sidewalk. We didn't have to wait long. The police arrived within ten minutes. I could hear the police asking them who had brought them here. The humans replied that they didn't even know who we were and that we had just left. We were grateful that they didn't point out our location in the bushes.

The police piled them into police cars and after ten minutes of fussing about, they drove away, leaving behind a cloud of dust.

My father placed an arm around me and my mother. He planted a kiss on each of our heads before saying, "Now it's time for us to go home."

Chapter 34: Rose

The familiar sight of The Shade's Port sent a warm feeling rushing through me.

We're home.

I could breathe freely for what felt like the first time since leaving our island. After all that had happened this past year, I swore to never take this place for granted again.

It being still early in the morning, most people would likely be asleep.

"Corrine, Ibrahim," my father said, his voice quiet. "Why don't you treat those among us who need it before turning in for the night?"

"Who needs medical attention?" Corrine asked, looking around each of us.

I looked down at my own chest. It was still red, but it wasn't really bothering me anymore. I supposed that it was best to get treated just in case it developed into something worse.

Most of the vampires chose to do without help, saying that they would be fine and their bodies would heal themselves after some nourishment. Kiev seemed to be the most seriously injured of the vampires, but Mona said that she would be able to treat him at home. In the end, it was just me, Micah, my grandfather, and Ashley who went to see Corrine and Ibrahim. Caleb accompanied me as we headed to their home.

I waited in line for my turn, and then lay down on Corrine's kitchen table, which she had turned into a treatment bed. She applied a cold compress to my chest and shoulders that stung momentarily.

"Nothing serious," she said.

After five minutes, she allowed me to sit up. I looked down at my skin. It was tinged slightly pink, but otherwise it was pretty close to its usual color.

"Thank you," I said.

"Caleb, how about you?" she asked. "You don't need any help?"

"I will be all right," he said. "The injuries I sustained have mostly healed themselves already."

"All right. The two of you should go and get some rest," she said, even as she yawned.

Caleb and I left the Sanctuary and began making our way through the forest. As we neared the Residences, we came across my parents standing with Vivienne and Xavier in the middle of the path.

I ran up and flung my arms around my aunt.

"Rose!" she said, hugging me back tightly. I felt the bump in her stomach.

Then I hugged my uncle.

"Your parents have just been telling us about your adventures," Vivienne said, smiling.

Adventures. Huh. That's one way to put it.

"Let's return to our apartment," my mother said, "where we can all sit comfortably and catch up."

Although I was exhausted, and my body wanted nothing more than to fall into bed and sleep, I was too curious to find out what had been happening around the island since we had been gone. So Caleb and I joined them in returning to my parents' penthouse. We all gathered in the living room, taking seats on the sofa.

We spent the next three hours recounting everything from our visit to the Blood Keep to our battle with the black witches. Once we had told all there was to tell, my father asked, "How have things been around here?"

"Suspiciously peaceful," Xavier said. "There is nothing much to report at all."

"What about the dragons?" I asked, still anxious about

our newly arrived residents.

"They've kept to themselves mostly," Vivienne said. "At least, none of them have come to see us. But I've heard through the grapevine—from Becky, that is—that they have all chosen girls now… except for the prince."

"Huh?" I jolted in my seat. "Theon still hasn't chosen a girl?"

Vivienne shook her head. "Nope."

"But… the main purpose of their stay was to find a partner for him, to continue their royal lineage. The other dragons' finding mates was supposed to be secondary."

Vivienne shrugged. "I'm not sure why he hasn't hooked up with anyone. Becky didn't seem to know either."

I wondered what this meant for us. If the prince saw nobody fit for him here, would they all leave?

"Don't worry about it now, honey," my mother said, squeezing my knee. "We'll find out what the situation is soon enough."

We talked for about an hour more, by which point I was no longer able to keep my eyelids open. They began to droop without me even realizing it. Caleb scooped me up in his strong arms and moved toward the door.

"Excuse us," he said.

"Good night," my family called after us as we left the apartment.

More like good morning, I thought groggily, before falling asleep in Caleb's arms.

Chapter 35: Rose

I woke to the sound of Caleb's light breathing next to me. I opened my eyes slowly, turning to face him on the pillow. He was still fast asleep.

Trying not to wake him, I gently lifted his right arm from over my waist and placed it down on the bed. Then I slid out from beneath the sheets and headed straight to the bathroom. I washed my face and brushed my teeth, then took a shower and washed my hair. It was shocking how much gunk had managed to stick in it. The pool of water forming on the shower floor was a murky brown.

After I'd finished in the shower, I grabbed a towel and wrapped it around me before heading back into the bedroom to get dressed. I was about to open my closet when the digital alarm clock on the windowsill caught my attention.

11.34 AM.

But it wasn't those blinking figures that made me stop. It was the date beneath them. I dropped my towel and picked up the clock, looking at it more closely in case I'd misread it.

I hadn't.

Wow. I'd completely lost track of time.

In just one day, it would be my birthday. My and Ben's birthday.

I had not been aware of the date for a while now, since so many things had happened one after the other. I just could not believe an entire year had gone by since Ben and I had plotted our escape to Hawaii.

"Nice view…" Caleb spoke huskily from the bed.

He'd woken up. Propping up his head with one hand, he was leaning on his elbow as his brown eyes roamed me.

I smirked, motioning to pick up my towel from the floor, but he grabbed me before I had the chance.

Trailing his hands from beneath my shoulders down to the base of my spine, he gathered me to him. His legs entwined with mine as he ran his nose down the bridge of mine before tasting my lips.

"What are you looking so surprised about, beautiful?" he asked in a whisper.

"I didn't realize how much time has passed... It's my birthday tomorrow."

He sat up. "You'll be eighteen."

Eighteen. It seemed so old.

Thinking back on my seventeenth year, I realized it was basically just one long blur of shocks, confusion, kidnappings and... Caleb.

I also couldn't believe that I was about to experience a birthday without Ben. It would be the first time we'd been apart on our birthday since the day we were born. A hollow feeling settled in at the base of my stomach.

I gulped.

I didn't want to start getting teary in front of Caleb, so I changed the subject.

"When is your birthday?" I asked.

"Not for a while," he said vaguely. "Let's talk about yours first... I have an idea for what we could do to celebrate."

I raised a brow.

He bent down close to me again, kissing my cheek and then whispering into my ear: "Let's get married, Rose."

I almost choked.

"Caleb... that would be the best birthday present. Ever."

Chapter 36: Caleb

After Rose responded to my suggestion with passion, I got off her, picked up her towel from the floor and handed it to her.

"If we're really going to have our wedding tomorrow, we've got to get a move on." She finished towel-drying her hair and put on a pair of jeans and a t-shirt. "Let's go see my parents."

"I have something to do," I said. She looked at me curiously, but didn't question what this something was. "You go without me."

"How long do you think you'll be?" she asked. "Because we need to decide on details about the wedding."

"Rose," I said, "we could hold the wedding in a cave,

and I wouldn't care." I gave her a smile. "Just make sure you show up."

"Okay," she said, grinning. "I'll try to remember that part. My mom, Corrine and I will do all the planning." She walked up to me and pulled my head down for another passionate kiss. "I'm going to be so busy, plus I'll be spending the night at my parents' place, we're unlikely to see each other again before tomorrow."

"Then I'll see you at the aisle."

Her cheeks flushed. "Yes," she said.

Embracing one more time, we said goodbye and she left the room. I watched through the window as she left, chuckling as she raced down the mountain and sprinted into the woods at full speed.

Now, I had my own preparations to see to.

I took a quick shower, got dressed and left the cabin. I made my way down the mountain, whipping through the trees until I reached the Sanctuary. I listened at the door before knocking, wondering if Corrine and Ibrahim might still be sleeping. I heard voices coming from within so I went ahead and rapped on the door.

It was Corrine who answered. Her hair was tied up in a messy bun and she wore a short nightgown.

"Hi, Caleb. What brings you here?"

"Is Ibrahim around?" I asked.

"Yes. Why?" She looked at me curiously, and then a

mischievous glint showed in her eyes. "Is this to do with Rose again?"

She knew me too well.

"Yes," I said. "You know it's her birthday in one day."

"Oh, my gosh. No. I've been totally oblivious to the days passing. I-I can't believe it's come round again so soon!"

"Yes, well… I need Ibrahim's help with something. It shouldn't take up much of his time."

"Okay," she said. She turned around and called back through her home. "Ibrahim!"

A deep groan emanated from one of the chambers. "I'm sleeping."

Corrine smirked and rolled her eyes. "No, you're talking," she shot back. "Get your butt out of bed. It's important. You can go back to sleep later."

I felt guilty as Ibrahim appeared at the door two minutes later. He wore pajamas, his hair was ruffled and he still had sleep in his eyes. Corrine squeezed his cheek before leaving the two of us alone.

"Hello, Caleb," he said.

"I'm sorry. I didn't want to disturb you—"

"It's all right," he said, stretching out and yawning. "What's the matter?"

I began to explain what I had in mind, and by the end, the warlock was nodding.

"Sounds easy enough," he said. "I can definitely help you with that. Come inside while I take a shower."

He led me into their living room where I waited while Ibrahim got ready. Then the two of us left for one of the more remote parts of the island where we were least likely to be seen. Ibrahim helped me with what he could in the space of an hour, and after that, I was able to continue without him.

Darkness had fallen beyond The Shade's boundary by the time I was satisfied with the result. I stopped by the ocean to splash my face with water before heading back to our cabin. I was expecting to find the place empty, since Rose had already informed me she wouldn't be returning that night.

I certainly wasn't expecting to find a dragon lurking in the shadows of our doorstep.

Chapter 37: Rose

As I made my way toward my parents' penthouse, I couldn't help but wonder what Caleb wanted to do. I could only assume that *something* was a surprise.

I knocked on the front door and my mother opened it after thirty seconds.

"Rose," she said, giving me a huge smile, "you do realize that it's your birthday tomorrow?"

Of course, Mom would remember my birthday even if the sky was falling.

"Yeah, I just realized this morning."

She took my hand and pulled me inside. "How do you want to celebrate?"

"Not another trip to Hawaii, I hope," my father said

dryly, looking up from a pile of papers as he sat at the breakfast table.

"Not quite," I said. Mention of that particular escapade made me wince. "Caleb and I want to get married."

That knocked both of them speechless.

"Oh," my mother said, her mouth hanging open.

My father dropped the piece of toast he was eating.

"What?" I said, amused by their reaction. "You already know Caleb and I are engaged."

"Oh, I think it's a good idea," my mother said quickly. "It's just… We weren't expecting it to happen so soon."

My father didn't say anything as I took a seat at the table next to him. He just stared at me. Although he didn't betray a lot of emotion in his expression, I could sense that he was crestfallen.

"Come on, Dad. You knew it was going to happen sometime." I reached out and squeezed his arm. "And I promise, I will always be your little girl… even when I'm eighty years old."

He rolled his eyes and I was relieved when he finally gave me a grin.

"And don't ever forget it," he said.

My mother looked up at the clock on the wall. "We've lost the morning already. That leaves us only the rest of the day to prepare for the wedding… That said, this island seems to have developed a tradition of last-minute weddings. We'll pull it off."

"Where are you going to hold it?" my father asked.

I paused. I hadn't really given the location much thought until now. "How about in the forest? You know that clearing near Grandpa's apartment—that would be large enough to fit a gazebo and as for the chairs and banquet table, we could position them among the trees. I think it would be beautiful."

"I love that idea," my mother replied. "And your dress, have you thought about it? I wish that you could have worn my wedding dress. It was so gorgeous."

"What happened to it?" I asked.

"I don't know. Honestly, this island has been through so much turmoil, it got lost at some point—perhaps when the Elders took over and many of the penthouses got destroyed."

"Well, we'll just have to design a new one," I said.

I fetched a notepad and pen. My mother and I spent the next half hour sketching out ideas before we finally came up with the final design.

She beamed at me. "Let's take this to Corrine... and then we need to start spreading the word to make sure more people than just your father and I show up."

CHAPTER 38: CALEB

"Theon?" I called up, stopping in my tracks and looking him over.

He bowed his head slightly, his amber-gold eyes fixed on me.

"What brings you here?" I asked, moving closer.

"I'd like to speak with you," he said, his voice calm.

I climbed up the steps to the porch and stopped a few feet away from him. "I'm listening."

"That one's special," he said.

There was a pause as I wondered what exactly his angle was. "Yes," I said. "Rose is special."

"There aren't many like her."

"There certainly aren't," I replied, holding his gaze

steadily. *You're preaching to the choir, dragon.*

"I trust you will treat her right."

I frowned at him. "I'm not sure I understand the purpose of your visit."

Closing the small distance between us, he motioned to touch my shoulder but stopped, his hand hovering midair. "May I?"

I looked from his hand to his face. Then shrugged.

He closed his hand over my shoulder. As we were practically the same height, his eyes were level with mine as they stared straight at me.

Of all the crazy experiences I'd had in my long life, this turned into one of the most bizarre. His pupils dilated and the amber of his irises became more brilliant. Although I had no intention of breaking eye contact, I had a strange feeling that I couldn't have averted my gaze even if I had wanted to. The intensity of his stare felt like he was digging a hole right through my pupils and carving out a tunnel through to my soul.

But whatever he was trying to see in me, I wasn't afraid. He could challenge me about my worthiness of Rose's love, but I knew what I felt for her. I had nothing to hide. He could rip right through to my soul and he would see that I held nothing but devotion for that woman.

I wasn't sure how much time passed, but it felt like at least five minutes before his eyes dimmed to their former color and he let go of my shoulder. He stepped away from me, though he still held my gaze.

Silence fell between us as I looked back at him, unflinching.

"Well?" I said. "Did you see all that you wanted to see?"

"I saw more than enough," he said quietly. "But, admittedly, it was not what I'd hoped to see… Vampire, you have a strong heart. Stronger than I'd thought. If there is anyone deserving of that woman other than a dragon, it is you."

He stepped back further, moving toward the steps.

"I bow out, with respect." Without another word, he turned on his heel and strode off into the night.

Well. That was strange.

I remained staring in his direction long after he'd disappeared, trying to make sense of what had just happened.

Still unsure of whether there was anything to draw from the experience, or perhaps even some reason to feel offended by it, I turned my back on the night and entered the cabin.

Whatever the case, even if nothing else, it would make a good tale to tell our children one day. That I had passed the test of the artist of romance, the dragon prince himself.

Chapter 39: Rose

Corrine was over the moon to work on my dress. We spent the rest of the day fixing my outfit, making arrangements for the venue, and then organizing invitations. All throughout, I kept thinking back to what Caleb was doing, but I didn't have much time to ponder.

I would've loved to go personally around the island to invite everyone, but instead Ashley, Becky, Abby and a few other classmates offered to do it. Rumors spread like wildfire among my peers, so I wasn't worried about the message making its way around the island.

Once I had finished all the tasks that I needed to be directly involved in, my mother returned with me to the penthouse. I washed off the subtle makeup we had applied during the dress rehearsal, and then my mother took me to my room and tucked me into bed, as she used to do when I was a child.

"Sweet dreams, my darling," she said, planting a kiss on my cheek.

"Good night, Mom. I love you."

"I love you too."

She gave me a watery smile before retreating out of the room. As her footsteps disappeared, I could have sworn that I heard a sob.

I tossed and turned that night, trying to fall asleep. My mind was just so alert. I was thinking about all the things that we had discussed today, and how everything was going to go tomorrow. But more than anything, I was thinking of Ben. How he should be sleeping in his bed further along the corridor. How I would have barged into his dark room early in the morning to wish him a happy birthday. How my mother would have cooked us both our favorite breakfast.

How he would miss my wedding.

Perhaps that had been the cause of my mother's sob.

***

The next morning went by so fast I could barely believe it. Before I knew it, I was staring at myself in the mirror, dressed in a gorgeous white gown that covered my feet, my hair flowing down my shoulders in soft curls.

Although I hadn't gotten much sleep, I was buzzing more than if I'd just shot myself up with ten cups of coffee.

Today's the day Caleb's going to make me his.

Everyone who'd been floating around the apartment helping with final preparations had now left for the venue. It was just my mother and I left in the apartment.

She approached behind me, running her hands down my arms and kissing my cheek.

"How are you feeling?"

"High," I murmured.

She chuckled.

"Is that how you felt when you married Dad?"

"Something like that... Are you ready to leave?"

"I think so."

I looped my arm through hers and we made our way out of the apartment, down the elevator and along the forest path. I could hear the chattering of a large crowd even from this distance. My palms began to grow sweaty—something I'd noticed a lot since I discovered my fire powers.

I suddenly had a horrible vision of my mascara melting from my body heat and dripping down my cheeks as I walked down the aisle.

"Is it usual to imagine everything that could possibly go wrong?"

"Yes," my mother said, giggling. "You're going to be

fine, honey. Before you know it, it will all be over. Just enjoy it while it lasts."

As we approached, I was taken aback by the sheer number of people who'd gathered for my wedding. I'd expected many to turn up, but not quite this many. For as far as I could see, chairs were spread out among the trees, all circling around the main gazebo that Corrine had set up. The gazebo was draped with light pink and white silk fabric and lined with roses, and it had been erected on a raised platform. Hanging back from the crowd, and standing on the path before us, were my father and my bridesmaids, Abby, Becky, Ariana and Ashley. The bridesmaids were dressed in matching lilac dresses.

I gave them all a weak smile.

As soon as my father laid eyes on me, he choked up. I said hello, but he didn't respond. He just nodded, his eyes sparkling. My mother, tears in her own eyes, took his hand and kissed his cheek before hugging me once more.

"Good luck," she said. "I'll see you on the other side…"

"Thanks," I croaked.

Ariana handed me a delicate bouquet of roses. Then I turned to my father. He held out his arm for me to take and I clasped it tight.

"Thank you," I whispered, "for being the best dad in the world."

He looked down at me, then shook his head. "No,

Rose," he said, his voice hoarse. "Thank you. I couldn't have wished for a braver, smarter, more beautiful daughter. I couldn't be prouder of you."

I felt my own eyes well with tears.

"Dammit, Dad. You're making me cry. My makeup is going to smudge."

"You don't need makeup anyway," he muttered, turning to face the gazebo.

From where I was standing, I couldn't yet see Caleb. We were standing a little aside from the aisle, so I couldn't see straight down it, and there were too many people still taking their seats.

Once everyone had settled and the chattering had died down, my bridesmaids walked around me and picked up the hem of my dress. I exchanged a final glance with my father before lowering my veil.

"Here we go…" he whispered.

I gripped my father's arm harder as we walked forward along the forest path and appeared at the end of the aisle. Straight ahead of me was the gazebo, under which stood Ibrahim—who usually took on the role of leading couples through the wedding ceremony—Micah, Caleb's best man, and right in the center, the man himself. The love of my life. Caleb Achilles.

Wherever Caleb had gone, I could see that Corrine had managed to make sure he looked presentable in her eyes.

He wore a gorgeous black tuxedo coupled with a crisp white shirt. His hair wasn't slicked back—it hung naturally, touching the sides of his handsome face—which was the way I liked it. I could see the warmth in his eyes even through my veil and from this distance. They were positively sparkling as he stared at me.

My face flushed. Heck, my whole body heated up.

My feet felt shaky, and I was glad to have such a strong support as my father.

"Almost there, darling," he whispered.

My heart racing, I barely noticed the guests. My eyes were fixed on the brown-eyed vampire who would soon own every part of me.

We neared closer and closer until we had arrived within five feet of him. Stretching out his arm and helping me up onto the platform, my father guided me toward Caleb and stepped back.

So close to Caleb now, I could make out every detail of his chiseled face. I felt grateful for the veil, because a stupid grin split my face as we locked eyes. It seemed to be contagious, because soon he was grinning too. Only he didn't have a veil to hide behind.

I tried to rein myself in. At every wedding I'd attended, the bride always smiled gracefully, not grinned like a fool. I felt like such a dork. Still, I couldn't help myself. Caleb just had that effect on me. He made me burst to life.

When it came time to exchange vows, my throat felt so dry I was sure that I'd sound like Lilith when I opened my mouth. I was glad that Caleb went first.

"Rose," Caleb began. His expression was serious now as he looked deep into my eyes. "When you collided with my world, I was afraid that you might break. I put all my efforts into locking you away, trying to shelter and hide you from danger. With time, it became clear that my fears were unfounded. You revel in adversity—it only makes you stronger, braver... more beautiful in my eyes. I want to wake up to your smile every day for the rest of my existence. You, Rose, are the one, the only one, for me. And I'm honored that you've chosen me as the one for you."

My grin had sure vanished by now. It was everything I could do to not let my emotions overwhelm me. The love I felt for this man was all-consuming. How could I even begin to articulate it?

"Caleb," I said. "If someone had told me exactly one year ago that I'd be walking down the aisle by the age of eighteen, I'd have laughed in their face. No other man could have made this happen but you, Caleb. Anyone who knew me then will agree. From our first encounter, I was drawn to you in a way I didn't even understand. But I knew that you were different than the company you kept. You didn't belong in that dark castle. It was during the time I spent between those cold stone walls that you captured my heart. So much so that it didn't matter when you returned me to The Shade. You still held me captive… Even though we haven't known each other long, it feels like you know me better than I know myself. You know when to reel me in and when to let me go. When to comfort and when to challenge me. And now, even though we've dealt with the black witches… I hope we'll find another crazy wave to ride together."

Caleb chuckled, beaming down at me.

We exchanged rings and then Ibrahim gave permission to "kiss the bride".

Caleb closed in on me, lifting my veil and reaching both hands behind my neck. Bending down to me, he pushed his lips against mine. He kissed me softly, slowly, allowing me to relish every second our lips touched. When he drew away, the crowd erupted in cheers.

Rose Achilles. That's who I am now.

"Rose, you're supposed to throw the bouquet," Micah whispered behind me.

I'd been too entranced with my new husband to think about what I should be doing. *Husband… I can hardly believe—*

"Throw the bouquet," Becky bugged.

Okay, okay.

Closing my eyes, I raised the bouquet over my shoulder and threw it blindly into the crowd. It looked like it was heading straight for Mona, but Helina leapt into the air and caught it just in time.

"I think it's time for a dance," Caleb said, placing his hands either side of my waist and leading me down the steps to the ground.

Everyone who had been seated on the chairs within the clearing stood up, and the witches moved them further into the trees, in order to create space for a dance floor.

A group of witches set up with instruments in one corner. I noticed Shayla among them, beginning to play the piano.

As Caleb began leading me in a dance, I thought back to our first encounter. *Dancing*. That was where everything had started for Caleb and me. If he hadn't arrived at that beach, and if Ben and I hadn't gone partying with Kristal and Jake, I likely never would've met this man. I never could have dreamed that night that this man would end up becoming my life partner. *How strange it is, how people come together.*

It was only now that I looked around more closely at the wedding attendees. I spotted Adelle and Eli standing at the edge of the dance floor, holding hands and talking. Micah and Kira had started dancing near us, and so had my grandfather and Kailyn. My mother and father were just about to join in along with Vivienne and Xavier.

"The ogres are here, too," Caleb said. He indicated with

his head to our right.

Brett and Bella were sitting on the ground with overflowing plates of food on their laps. Food had not even been served yet, so I could only assume they had helped themselves. A smile spread across my face as I realized that they had dressed up. Brett wore a large white shirt and—shock, horror—pants. I was so used to him wearing a loin cloth, I had to look twice to check I wasn't seeing things. Bella on the other hand wore a long cream smock that reached beneath her knees. Though cross-legged on the ground, she was not sitting at the most strategic of angles. She was flashing her underwear to everyone who looked her way. Which was probably why nobody was looking her way.

Corrine must have attacked them both with a wardrobe. Not the best choice of colors, though. Their smart-looking clothes were fast being soiled as they overfilled their mouths with wedding food.

At least they looked like they were enjoying themselves.

"Happy birthday, Rose!" Griffin called to me. He swerved next to us, dancing with Becky.

"Thank you." I laughed, even as joy mixed with melancholy.

"Happy birthday, Rose," Anna and Kyle called, also taking to the dance floor.

"Thank you," I said again, giving them a smile.

I noticed Ariana in one of the seats looking after baby Kiev.

I continued looking around and greeting people. I was amazed at the turnout with such short notice. I couldn't spot a single dragon anywhere, though. I guessed that they were still feeling sore that their prince couldn't have me. Otherwise, the only familiar faces I couldn't spot were Yuri and Claudia. It saddened me that they weren't here, but I knew that I could count on them to be having lots of fun in Paris.

We danced for about half an hour more, and then it was time to cut the cake. Corrine floated it into the center of the dance floor on a table and beckoned to Caleb and me to approach. Laced with white and light pink icing, it was a gorgeous cake. I felt almost bad cutting it. Holding the knife together, Caleb and I sliced a piece.

As was custom, Corrine insisted that we take the first bite. Unfortunately, Caleb couldn't or it would make him feel sick. He picked up the piece of cake and dug a spoon into it, feeding me.

He smiled, watching my reaction. "Good?"

I nodded, licking my lips. It was delicious. We moved to a seat at the side of the dance floor and Caleb pulled me onto his lap. He spoon-fed me the rest of the cake, watching me with interest as I swallowed.

"Don't you miss dessert?" I asked.

"You're all the sugar I need." He winked at me.

I reached my fingers through his hair and ruffled it, winking back.

After Corrine and Ibrahim had finished dishing out the entire cake to our guests, they began serving the main course.

The piece of cake Caleb had fed me was particularly large, and I wasn't hungry for anything else, so Caleb and I entered the dance floor again while everyone was busy with lunch. I enjoyed having the area to ourselves. I draped my arms around his neck, resting my head against his chest and listening to his heartbeat. I closed my eyes, blocking out the rest of the world, locking myself in our own little bubble.

When people finished eating many took to the dance floor again. The music sped up and became more lively. I enjoyed Caleb walking me through the different moves at various paces. I even tried a few moves of my own— something I didn't usually do with him since he was so expert at leading me. As I did a little twirl, Caleb paused, looking at me with raised brow.

"Getting a bit adventurous, aren't we?"

I snorted, before doing another twirl. I definitely felt more confident at dancing now than a year ago—all credit to Caleb. At least, I didn't feel like such a klutz.

"Why don't you try leading me?" he asked, taking my waist again.

"Leading you… into embarrassment?"

He laughed. "Just give it a try."

"Okay."

As the music picked up pace, I took the lead. It was surprisingly effortless. I was so used to mirroring Caleb, flowing with music came naturally to me now. I barely thought about it.

"I'm impressed," he said.

"Well… you're a good teacher."

More people joined us on the dance floor again once lunch was over and we continued dancing for hours. I'd long lost track of how much time had passed, but I knew it must have been a lot because my feet were beginning to ache. Kicking off my shoes, I continued barefoot.

Then it was time for my presents. My mother approached us and pointed to the seats where a pile of wrapped gifts were stacked. I felt bad to see how large it was. I sat down and began unwrapping them one by one. My parents had gotten me a brand new phone. Vivienne and Xavier gave me an e-reader pre-loaded with dozens of my favorite novels. I opened Ibrahim and Corrine's package to find my passport, reverted to its original state with my real date of birth. I looked up at Corrine guiltily. Also in the package was a collection of intoxicating perfume— apparently hand-crafted by Corrine.

My grandfather's package was oddly shaped. Ripping it

open, I found that I was holding a long silver dagger enclosed within a gold-encrusted sheath.

"Wow," I muttered, sliding out the shiny blade. "This is badass, Grandpa."

Everyone laughed. "It took some time convincing your mother to allow me to give you that." Aiden chuckled. "But I think you've shown us all you're more than capable of wielding a weapon… Just be careful not to cut your finger as you slide it back in."

I wasn't ready to put the dagger away yet though. I used it to open the next present: Griffin's gift. I sliced through the wrapping paper to reveal a massive bag of pig-shaped chocolates. I burst out laughing. "Back to the piggies this year, eh, Griff? You always know how to please a girl."

Griffin threw me a wink.

Eli had gifted me… a clunky calculator. I looked up at him, smiling and wondering if it was a joke.

He grinned. "That's no ordinary calculator. Trust me, it'll make calculus homework more interesting."

Okay…

Micah's package contained a pair of pearl earrings while Anna's family had gifted me an oil painting depicting a view of The Shade's port.

"We all painted that together," Ariana said. "Except my baby brother, of course."

I was speechless. I wanted to run back to Caleb's and my

cabin and stick it on the wall right away. It was a painting I knew I'd treasure forever.

Within Kiev—who'd turned back into himself by now—and Mona's box was a blue gemstone necklace and when I reached for the next parcel, Brett called from my right.

"Open this one next."

I turned to see him milling through the crowd, holding a large object covered by white fabric—fabric I soon realized was the white shirt Brett had been wearing earlier.

"Oh, thanks Brett," I said, as he dumped the object at my feet.

"It's from Bella, too." He nodded over his shoulder toward the ogress, who was still wearing the smock Corrine had fixed her up with—rather stained by now.

I stood up and unwrapped the object from Brett's giant shirt. I found myself looking down at a dark wooden chair. It had pretty carvings around its base and, when I sat down on it, it was surprisingly comfortable.

"Thank you so much, Brett and Bella."

Brett grinned from ear to ear before making his way back toward Bella.

Most of the other gifts consisted of beautiful handmade jewelry and clothes, gorgeous artwork and more chocolates. By the time I'd finished opening all of them, my right wrist felt sore.

I looked around at the crowd of family, friends and well-wishers surrounding me and said thank you for what felt like the hundredth time.

Wherever you are, Ben, I hope you're having a good birthday too. Or, at least, a safe one.

Now that the gift-opening ceremony was over, many people retreated to the dance floor or seats further away.

Caleb leaned in toward me.

"It's almost midnight. I still haven't given you a birthday present."

"You are my birthday present, Caleb," I said, kissing his cheek.

"Maybe… but come."

Intrigued, I slid my hand in his and he began leading me away from the clearing. I caught sight of Abby and Erik making out beneath a tree. They barely noticed us as we passed by.

My father, who was leading my mother in a slow dance, caught my eye.

"See you tomorrow," he said, a knowing look on his face.

My mother looked toward us too and waved.

I nodded, feeling myself blush a little.

Anticipation was starting to light up my body as we moved further and further away from the crowds, becoming more and more alone. I couldn't walk well in my dress, so once we had reached the main forest path, Caleb scooped me up in his arms and carried me.

We were about to leave the area completely when a figure stirred in the trees.

"Who is that?" I whispered.

Stepping out from the shadows was none other than Theon. Apparently, he had been witnessing the festivities from afar.

His brilliant amber eyes fixed on me. Caleb put me down on my feet. The dragon towered over me as I stepped toward him.

"Hello, Theon. How are you?"

He only nodded in response.

"We heard that you never picked a girl in the end."

"You heard correctly," he said, glancing briefly at Caleb before looking back to me.

"How come?" I asked. "Was no one here to your liking? We have plenty of ladies here on this island—"

"You have many fair and worthy maidens on this island," he said. "But none are meant for me." His smooth baritone voice only added to his calm demeanor.

"Oh," I said, taken aback. "Then… what will you do?"

"I leave early tomorrow," he said.

"Leave? Where will you go?"

"On a journey," he replied.

"A journey to where?"

"To find a female capable of bearing my love."

I paused. "Will you, uh, stay within this human realm?"

He nodded.

"You said before that you don't go looking for partners yourself. That it's your comrades' job. Will they leave with you?"

"No. I have ordered them to remain here… It's become clear that my lineage's customs must be set aside in this case." He paused, his eyes becoming distant as he raised his gaze toward the trees. The moonlight trickled down through the canopy of leaves, casting shadows upon the shifter's tan, muscled chest that was partially covered with a thin cloth draped over his left shoulder. The silence of the forest surrounded us, the chattering of the party far away. A gentle breeze blew against our skin.

When he finally broke the silence, his gaze was still unfocused, his voice husky. "The wind is calling… and I must answer to it."

I exchanged glances with Caleb, who shrugged.

"Well, perhaps one day we'll see you again."

"Perhaps." His gaze lowered to my face, his eyes digging deep into mine one last time before he bowed his head slightly and disappeared into the night.

We remained rooted to our spots a few moments longer, staring toward the direction the dragon had retreated. Then Caleb reached for my hand. "Shall we proceed?"

CHAPTER 40: ROSE

My husband picked me up again and sped up along the forest path. Soon, we had exited the woods and neared the shore. When we arrived at the Port, he set me down on my feet again. Then he stepped in front of me, blocking my view of the jetty.

"Close your eyes," he whispered.

I did as he'd requested. He moved behind me, pulling my back against his chest. He placed one wide palm over my eyes to make sure I didn't peek, while he rested the other one over my stomach. He walked forward with me, guiding me in my long dress and making sure that I didn't slip. The floorboards creaked beneath us and after what felt like twenty feet, he drew us both to a stop.

"Keep your eyes closed until I say. I'm going to let go of you."

"Okay."

I had to fight the urge to not sneak a peek.

When Caleb finally did give me permission, I gasped.

Floating on the waves before me was a gorgeous boat. About fifteen feet long and ten feet wide, its frame was made of dark brown timber. There were four masts in each corner from which hung long drapes of crimson silk. The floor was padded with soft cushioned material and scattered with mahogany-red pillows. Candles lined the edges of the boat, making it glow in the darkness and look almost... unearthly.

Watching my face closely, Caleb stepped into the boat. Holding out a hand, he whispered:

"Sail away with me, Princess."

My hand was unsteady as I reached out and closed my fingers around his.

He led me to the center of the boat and left me there while he moved back to the bow and cut us loose from the jetty. The boat began to drift, the calm waves carrying us away.

Caleb turned back to face me, gazing at me through his dark lashes. Positioning three cushions on the floor, he seated me on them before picking up a pair of oars that had been resting near the stern. He removed his jacket, sat opposite me and began to row.

I couldn't tear my gaze away from him as he moved us away, the muscles beneath his white shirt rippling with each stroke he took.

He stopped once we neared the boundary of the island and I could no longer make out details of the Port in the distance.

He set the oars to one side, then knelt next to me. I propped myself up on my knees as he gathered me to him. He touched the back of my neck, his fingers reaching into my hair, before claiming my lips and kissing me deeply. I closed my eyes, returning his passion.

My breathing was fast and uneven as he drew away. He stood up and pulled me up with him. The top buttons of his shirt were open, his hair tousled from the sea breeze and all the dancing we'd done. His appearance reminded me of the night he'd proposed.

Caleb Achilles… My gorgeous sailor husband.

"You didn't have to do this," I said, finding my voice for the first time.

He just smiled.

Taking my hand in one hand, he reached the other around my back, gently pressing me against him. We began to sway to the music in our heads.

I shivered when he moved his hand to the strap of my wedding dress. He rolled it slowly down my shoulder before lowering his head to kiss the skin it had been covering. The feel of his lips so close to my neck made my stomach flutter. His mouth caressed me tenderly, unhurriedly, as though we had all the time in the world. Then he reached for my second strap and pulled it aside. Still swaying my body gently, he began kissing my shoulder with as much tenderness and devotion as he had done the first.

My body was beginning to course with heat I didn't know how to contain. I raised my hands to the opening of his shirt and fumbled with the buttons.

His hands found the zipper running down the back of my dress. I felt the coldness of the metal slide down my skin as he released me from the gown. It slid to the floor, leaving me standing in my underwear.

As I undid the last of his shirt buttons, he pulled the shirt off and dropped it on the floor near my dress. I let my gaze roam over the beauty of Caleb's physique before locking eyes with him again.

Deftly, he unclasped my bra. Then he got down on his knees and bared me to him completely.

I watched in anticipation as he finished undressing himself. Slowly, we stepped toward each other, meeting again in the center of the boat. The way his bare skin touched and brushed against mine was electrifying. Surrounding me with his strong arms, he pulled me flush against him.

I felt his need.

Caressing my earlobe with his lips, he breathed against my ear:

"May I take you, Rose?"

My throat felt so tight, I could hardly speak. "Yes," I managed.

"All of you?"

"All of me."

Kissing the side of my face, he ran his wide palms down the back of my thighs and lowered me to the floor. As I lay beneath him, my head against the pillows, he knelt over me, gazing down at me for several moments before dipping down.

He kissed my lips, then my neck and the base of my throat. His kisses trailed down the center of my chest, over my ribcage, my stomach, and down to my abdomen. I wasn't sure how much longer I could hold out when his mouth found my inner thigh. My chest heaving, I bit down hard on my lower lip.

He moved back up my body so that his face was level with mine, his mouth once again closing around my lips. I gripped his hair, pulling him closer.

Then his hips pressed against me.

And he took me.

All of me.

Even as we made love, it felt like a dance. A dance I didn't need to learn.

His tongue brushed against mine in rhythm to the rest of his body, our breathing forming a symphony as he explored the deepest part of me.

The lapping of the waves, the blowing of the wind, the flickering of the candlelight, even the stars glimmering overhead seemed to join in the beat of our love.

I still didn't know what lay ahead of us, how we would make what we had last. Whether I would risk turning into a vampire, or Caleb would turn into a human.

But we had time.

Caleb was mine and I was his.

And as our hearts beat against each other, the heat of my body melding with the coolness of his, nothing else in the world mattered.

Chapter 41: Sofia

Derek and I turned in soon after Rose left with her new husband. There were too many gifts to carry back with us, so Corrine offered to transport them to Rose's bedroom in our penthouse by magic.

Leaving the area, Derek and I didn't speak much as we headed back home. We walked hand in hand, lost in our own thoughts.

Arriving at the front door, we headed straight for our bedroom. I entered the bathroom and started brushing my teeth. Derek pushed open the door a moment later to join me. I caught his eye in the mirror. I was expecting to see moroseness in his expression—after all, this was the first night Rose was officially Caleb's. Instead, the corners of his lips were curved up in a smile.

I raised a brow, my mouth filled with toothpaste.

He responded by burying his head against the back of my neck and kissing me.

"I was just thinking of our wedding night," he said, resurfacing.

Ah. That should be reason enough to smile… Then again, I recalled how much anxiety we'd been in, since Derek had been due to take the cure the very next day and neither of us had had any idea whether or not it would work.

I rinsed out my mouth.

"I said to Rose how much better behaved Caleb has been with her than you were with me." I gave him a teasing smile.

He placed his hands on my hips, pulling me back against him. "But would you have had it any other way?"

I craned my neck up to kiss him full on the mouth. "You know I wouldn't."

We changed into our night clothes and got into bed. Though there really wasn't much point in changing into clothes with Derek giving me his look. We'd stripped out of them in a matter of seconds.

After we'd finished our tumble in bed, I nestled my head against him while he brushed his fingers through my hair.

We both sighed.

"A daughter married," I said. "A son missing. What a

year it's been."

"Barely an hour goes by when I don't think of Ben," Derek said, "but… I'm not as worried about him as I was before."

My eyes shot up toward him. "Why?"

He paused before replying. "After seeing Rose's growth in the face of danger while she was away from The Shade, whatever Ben is going through now, I can only think that he will pull through it stronger and braver than ever before."

I wanted nothing more than for my son to return. But I couldn't deny that Derek's words had struck a chord with me. Although Rose's gumption scared the living daylights out of me sometimes, I couldn't have been prouder of her.

Gradually, I'd also been coming to terms with why Ben had chosen to leave. Even after hours of discussion with Derek about it, I still hadn't accepted why our son had seen no other option.

But Ben was prince of The Shade. He'd killed Yasmine. An innocent young woman. One of his people, his citizens, who'd looked up to him as an authority. As a ruler.

Ben had done what any true leader would do—held himself accountable and taken full responsibility for his actions. He didn't want to return until he was certain such an incident would never occur again.

As his mother, I'd lost perspective. I realized that I

should be proud of him for making that decision, despite the pain it caused me. Ben was a stronger man than I'd given him credit for.

"I agree with you, Derek," I said. "Adversity will be good for our son."

Derek looked surprised. He'd probably been expecting me to disagree with him and try to persuade him once again that we ought to go looking for Ben.

My husband raised a brow.

I propped myself up on my elbow and looked him in the eye.

"Because that's how heroes are made."

Epilogue: Ben

I stared down at the mark of a black cross etched into my right bicep.

Who did this?

I got to my feet and looked around my bedroom, scanning it for any sign of someone having entered. I couldn't spot anything out of place. I sniffed the air. I was familiar by now with Jeramiah's scent, but I couldn't detect it. I walked out of the bedroom and entered the dark corridor outside. I headed straight for the front door at the other end of it. No sign of forced entry, that was for sure. Of course, whoever had done this would have had a key.

I returned to the doorway of my bedroom and stood there, looking over the luxurious Egyptian furnishings. I was still coming to terms with the fact that I'd been drugged. Heavily, to not have woken up while my skin was being inked.

I glanced down at the tattoo again. It was beginning to prickle less. I wondered how long ago it had been done. For all I knew, it could've been just minutes before I woke up.

One thing was clear: I'd been right in my instinct to not trust these people.

Unwilling to just sit about my apartment now that I'd woken, I opened the front door and stepped out. I looked up and down the terrace outside. It was empty. I could hear deep breathing coming from the apartments surrounding me. I also couldn't hear any noises coming from the desert above. They must have finished up their festivities by now and retreated to their rooms.

I was about to turn right and begin making my way around the atrium when I caught sight of a girl on the terrace opposite me. She was slumped on a bench, a bottle of wine in her hand. Her complexion was white, and as I looked closer, I realized that she was Jeramiah's half-blood girlfriend. Marilyn. She was drunk out of her mind. Her head lolled back against the wall. She was muttering inaudibly to herself, and I couldn't be sure whether she had noticed me or not. I walked swiftly forward, acting as if I hadn't noticed her.

While most people seemed to be sleeping after a night of

drinking, I wanted to take this opportunity to explore this place at my own pace, without Jeramiah's gaze on me. I doubted it would bring me any closer to discovering who had branded me, of course. For that, I'd have to wait until people started waking.

Avoiding the elevator, I walked down a flight of stairs to the level beneath me. I circled the entire level, trying a few doors behind which I couldn't hear snoring, but most were locked. Jeramiah had said that the apartments on these levels were the quarters of vampires and witches in any case. I imagined they'd look much the same as my and Jeramiah's apartments. I descended level after level in the atrium until I reached the ground floor. Mixing with the sweet aroma of jasmine, the scent of human blood was strong. Strong enough to cause my mouth to water, even though I had only recently topped up on blood.

Clenching my jaw, I moved toward the room I had waited in while Jeramiah had disappeared with the human I'd half-turned, Tobias. I approached the door, clutching the handle and expecting it to be locked. It wasn't. I was able to push it wide open and step inside the dark, bare room. My eyes fixed on the door at the opposite side of the room that Jeramiah had carried Tobias through.

I was still afraid of my inability to control myself around fresh, hot blood. But this was a part of The Oasis I hadn't seen at all yet. I felt I needed to explore it at least once.

I breathed in deeply, trying to reel in my cravings, before reaching for the handle and twisting it.

This door was locked.

I looked around the room for a key. Never mind a key, there wasn't anything in this small, dusty room.

Bending down on my knees, I peered through the keyhole. This seemed to be a basic lock, nothing sophisticated. I was confident that I'd be able to pick it, if I had something long and sharp. I was unsure of where to start looking for a suitable object. Then I realized that I might be already be equipped with what I needed.

Looking down at my hands, I extended my claws. If this was going to work at all, the claw in my forefinger seemed to be the best fit for the job.

I inserted two claws through the keyhole and began to pick the lock. My claws worked surprisingly well. I'd been worried that they might be too thick. After a minute, I managed to get the door to click open.

If I was quick and didn't get caught by anyone already in the basement, nobody needed to know that I'd ventured down without permission.

The scent of blood intensified as I stepped through the door and found myself standing at the top of a narrow winding staircase. My gut clenched. I hoped that I wouldn't regret this decision.

Reaching the basement, I was met with a much less

primitive prison than I had imagined. Thanks to my foray into the territory of the black witches, I was used to dungeons being separated into cells by mere gates, with no bedding to sleep on or even clean water to drink.

This place, however, looked civilized, at least on first glance. I found myself standing at the end of a narrow corridor lined either side with doors. I peeked through the thin strip of window at the top of the first door to my left. I found myself looking into a small room with a bed, a sink, and even a door that apparently led to a toilet. It also looked relatively clean. A man who looked middle-aged was sleeping on the bed, a blanket pulled up to his neck. I kept moving, looking through window after window, hoping to find Tobias. It was clear that I was in the wrong section though. I could only smell human blood among these rooms, no half-blood.

Another thing that surprised me about this place was the fact that all of these humans seemed to have a room to themselves. One also wouldn't know that one was in the desert down here. It felt like there was some kind of air-conditioning system.

I didn't understand why they held such high standards for their prisoners. I wasn't used to seeing prisoners being treated like this by supernaturals. It was odd. Especially considering—I assumed—they only ended up using these humans for blood anyway.

I finished traveling along the corridor to meet with another door. This one was not locked. I pushed it open and continued walking forward. I could detect half-bloods now.

This area was lined with similar rooms, but they seemed to be bigger and had a more comfortable feel to them. More effort had been put into making these people feel at home. I noticed bookshelves in some of them, and even the occasional mini-fridge. I continued looking from chamber to chamber, passing half-bloods of all ages and genders. Finally, at the end of the long winding corridor, I found Tobias. It was impossible to tell what state he was in because he was fast asleep. Still, he was alive.

Now I just had to hope that his life wouldn't be worse here than if I had just let cancer claim him.

The area Tobias was in led to yet more corridors lined with rooms. I walked further for about five minutes, and still hadn't reached the end of them. I was shocked by just how many people they kept down here.

If someone came down, it would be impossible to avoid them. The corridors were narrow and there was nowhere to hide. I decided it was time to return upstairs even though I hadn't finished looking around.

Passing back along the various corridors, I climbed to the top of the stairs and walked back out into the small room where I had picked the lock. I closed the door behind me and, sliding my claw into the keyhole, I fiddled around with it again until it clicked shut.

Then I walked back out onto the terrace outside. Unsure of where to roam next, I found myself walking absentmindedly toward the lush gardens in the center of the atrium. I walked past the various exotic plants and flowers, barely appreciating their beauty and the effort it must have taken to grow them. My thoughts were lost elsewhere.

It was only when I passed by a pond covered with blue water lilies that something caught my eye. A stone slab, fixed into the ground at the edge of the water. It caught my eye because the grayness of it was so at odds with the lush surroundings. I strayed from the narrow path and crossed the grass to stand over it.

Even though I had perfect eyesight, I was convinced that I'd been imagining things.

But, as I bent right down close to the stone, there was no room for doubt.

Etched into the stone were the words:

"In memory of Lucas Dominic Novak."

My jaw dropped.

Lucas Novak?

Who on earth would have installed this here?

It had to have been done since this coven had arrived here. Jeramiah had already told me that they'd rebuilt this place from scratch.

Could it be possible that one of these vampires or witches used to be a friend of his and knew that The Oasis was where he had met his demise?

Shaken by the idea that I could be in the presence of a close acquaintance of my family, I headed straight back to my apartment. Whoever had erected this wouldn't be a well-wisher of my parents. Lucas and my father had been bitter enemies, and he had met his death at the hands of my grandfather while trying to murder my mother.

No friend of Lucas would be a friend of mine.

Locking the front door behind me, I headed back to my bedroom. I almost jumped as I laid eyes on a blonde girl sprawled out on my bed. Marilyn. She was naked but for a sheet pulled up to her chest. Still holding a bottle of wine in one hand, she looked up at me through hooded eyelids.

"Don't mind if I sleep here, do you?" she slurred.

"What are you doing? Where's Jeramiah?"

She scowled. "He said I drank too much tonight. Didn't want me in his apartment. Said I snore too much," she replied, before taking another swig from her bottle.

I snatched the bottle from her and shoved it out of reach.

Her frown deepened.

"You can't sleep here," I hissed. "Find a spare room in someone else's apartment."

Her lips formed a coy smile. "I'm not used to sleeping alone." I looked away as she sat up abruptly in bed, the sheet slipping to reveal her bare form.

Jesus Christ.

Keeping my eyes fixed on the door, I said through gritted teeth, "Get out. Now."

"If you're worried about Jeramiah, he doesn't mind really. He shares me all the time…"

He shares you, or you share yourself?

To my discomfort, she leapt out of bed and flung herself at me. I brushed her away, grabbing another sheet from the bed and wrapping it around her tightly so that her arms were trapped within it. I looked toward the door before turning back to face her. Her eyes were glassy and bloodshot.

"If you want to stay here, you're going to answer some of my questions," I said, my voice low.

"Sounds fair enough, I s'pose."

I sat her down on the bed, before leaning back against the wall, watching her intently.

I showed her the mark on my right biceps.

"Who did this?" I asked.

She eyed the tattoo. "I dunno. We all get them once we arrive here. I've got one too, see." She struggled to show me her tattoo, but failed miserably due to the tightness of the sheet around her.

"So one of you did this to me?"

She shrugged. "Who else would have done it?"

It was clear that she wasn't going to contribute much on this topic, so I changed the subject.

"Why is there a memorial stone by the lily pond for Lucas Novak?"

She frowned, as though struggling to understand what I'd said.

I asked the question again, slower this time.

"Stone," she slurred. "Oh, yeah. That old thing. I wondered the same thing when I saw Jeramiah clearing away the weeds from it one day."

"Jeramiah?" I leaned in closer.

"Yeah, my supposed boyfriend who kicks me out of his bed whenever he feels like it…"

"Tell me more," I urged, careful to keep my voice low.

"He also lies and says I talk too much when I've had too much to—"

"No! More about the memorial stone. You saw Jeramiah cleaning it. Was he the one who installed it by the pond?"

"Yeah… For his dad."

My voice caught in my throat.

"Dad?" I breathed.

"If you could call him that," she replied. "Jeramiah told me that he never even met his father. He doesn't even think that his father knew of his existence."

"H-How could that be?"

"Jeramiah said his father was..." She paused, smirking. "Let's just say that in his youth he wasn't great at keeping his pants on. Something I wish you weren't great at right now..." She cast me another longing glance before licking her lips and continuing. "Jeramiah's mother was the daughter of a poor mill owner. She was just sixteen when Lucas knocked her up. According to Jeramiah, she didn't realize that she was pregnant until two months later... but by then, Lucas was nowhere to be found. Moved on, I guess. Left town. Who the hell knows. Perhaps the Elder had even gotten him by then... Poor ol' Jera. His mother died when he was still young. And he's always had a chip on his shoulder for growing up as a bastard child. He never used Novak as his surname. Titled himself Jeramiah Stone."

My mind was one blur of confusion. A hundred conflicting questions and doubts crowded my head at once.

"How...How is this possible?" was all I managed to voice.

"How is what possible?" Her mood changed to irritation. "I don't get what's so surprising. The Elders are famous for tracking down members of the same bloodline. Once they found a lineage that worked for them, they'd try to snatch up as many blood relations as they possibly could. And the Novaks, apparently, were one of their favorite families. They targeted everyone who was even remotely related to a Novak. Apparently, that family always had a leaning towards darkness…" The obvious finally dawned on her. "Why are you so interested anyway? Did you know Lucas Novak?"

I shook my head. "No," I said truthfully. "I was just curious."

That seemed to be enough of an answer to direct her attention away from me in her drunken state.

"I have to leave," was the one thought circling my mind now.

This was just one bad omen too many.

I couldn't be sure whether Jeramiah knew that I was a Novak or not. But something had obviously drawn him to me. Whatever it was, I wasn't about to hang around to find out.

The son of Lucas Novak was someone I had to get as far away from as possible.

I looked around the room, forming a plan. I headed first for the closet by the bed and began emptying it of all the clothes I could find. Grabbing one shirt after the other, I pulled them over me until I had a thick layer of shirts covering my skin. Then I did the same with pants, though I was only able to pile on two pairs. I headed straight to the kitchen and opened the refrigerator. I was relieved to see containers of blood there. I emptied the fridge of the blood and tied the supply up in a bed sheet. Next, I searched the apartment for something that I could use to shield myself from the sun. I found an umbrella sitting on a shelf in a cupboard in one of the spare rooms. It looked flimsy, but it would have to do.

Making sure that the sheet was wrapped tightly around the blood, I picked it up and flung it over my shoulder. I took one last look around the bedroom to see if there was anything else I could possibly bring with me before heading toward the door.

"Where you going?" Marilyn asked, standing up and padding toward me. "What are you doing? Why don't you want to stay the night with me? I answered all your questions."

Ignoring her, I freed her from the sheet I'd tied around her before hurrying to the front door. I pulled it open and raced along the terrace toward the elevator leading up to the very top floor. Emerging beneath the trap door that led straight up to the desert, I climbed up the final set of stairs and pushed upward hard against the ceiling. It didn't budge.

Dammit.

As I remembered it, it had been a witch who'd opened it before.

I tried pushing against it once again with all my strength, and to my relief, this time, there was a crack and one of the doors pushed open. I winced at how much noise I'd made, but it couldn't be helped. I climbed up through the roof. A wave of heat engulfed me as I emerged in the desert. Beyond the boundary in the distance, the sun had already risen. Hence the need for all these extra layers and the umbrella to cover my skin.

Fortunately, I could run fast. And I had some blood to keep me going for a while. I just had to hope that there would be some settlement or sign of civilization not too far away.

Although I cursed myself for coming here in the first place, I could hardly blame myself. I'd been at the end of my tether, unable to see how I could stop attacking humans in broad daylight even while trying to keep myself stranded in the middle of the ocean in a submarine.

But now, even that situation seemed preferable to staying here. Everything about the atmosphere felt wrong. I couldn't stand to stay here even a moment longer.

It was a hive of my parents' enemies. My enemies.

After I'd taken the first steps away from the trap door, a sudden burst of pain shot through my right arm. It was emanating from my tattoo. I stopped, momentarily stunned. I pressed my left hand hard against my bicep, trying to soothe it. But that only made it more painful. I continued walking. The pain only increased until I was clenching my jaw against the pain and forcing myself forward with all the willpower I possessed.

Despite the agony and the heat of the almost-midday sun beating down beyond the boundary, I continued racing forward as fast as I could.

Just keep going.

I was sure that I had run at least one mile already. I remembered how Jeramiah had said to stay within five miles of the boundary to avoid hunters. I would have to hope to slip by them silently. Because staying wasn't an option.

After what felt like five miles, I was about to brace myself for the hunters when I slammed into an invisible barrier. I staggered back, staring in horror at the patch of sand I'd been unable to walk past.

My tattoo prickling more than ever, I moved further up and tried to pass through in a different spot. Still unsuccessful, I tried several more areas even further along and in different directions.

Each time, my attempts were in vain.

I was trapped.

WHAT'S NEXT?

Dear Shaddict,

So Caleb and Rose finally got their Happy Ever After.
Though their story has ended, The Shade has not!
From the ruins of the final battle, a new hero has emerged.
A hero who will take The Shade into unchartered territories.
Who will usher in a new world order, in which no predator may ever be safe again.
And who will experience and learn to love, like no man has ever done before…

A Shade of Vampire 17: A Change of Wind is available to order now.

Please visit www.bellaforrest.net for details.

Also, if you'd like to stay up to date about Bella's new releases, please visit: www.forrestbooks.com, enter your email and you'll be the first to know.

I can't wait to meet you back in The Shade!
Love,
Bella x

a wind of
change

A Shade of Vampire, Book 17

BELLA FORREST

A Note About Kiev

Dear Shaddict,

If you're curious about what happened to Kiev during his time away, how he met Mona and how he came upon Anna, I suggest you check out his completed stand-alone trilogy: *A Shade of Kiev.*

Kiev's story will also give you a deeper understanding of the Shade books and the kind of threat the Novaks have been up against.

Please visit my website for more details: www.bellaforrest.net

Best wishes,
Bella

Made in the USA
Lexington, KY
17 February 2016